DOWNSHIFT

DOWNSHIFT

MATT HUGHES

Doubleday Canada Limited

Canadian Cataloguing in Publication Data

Hughes, Matt
    Downshift

ISBN 0-385-25601-9

I. Title.

PS8565.U3397D66 1997   C813'.54   C96-932252-6
PR9199.3.H83D66 1997

Cover photograph by Ron Fehling
Cover design by Tania Craan
Text design by Heidy Lawrance Associates
Printed and bound in Canada

Published in Canada by
Doubleday Canada Limited
105 Bond Street
Toronto, Ontario
M5B 1Y3

For Linda Coady,
always a true friend.

One

"MYSTERY CORPSE IDD AS missing stock promoter,"
read the headline. The type was large enough to be scanned
from near-earth orbit, if any *Star Wars* hardware was trained
on my doorstep this mid-November morning in 1989. The
72-point screamer was zippered across the upper front
page of the local biweekly, which lay on top of the dailies
from Vancouver and Victoria.

I stooped, tucked the local under my arm and checked
the fronts of the big-city papers, but they were mainly
interested in the collapse of East Germany and the
growing chaos in the provincial government. There was
nothing about car and body parts scattered up on Mount
Washington.

I took all three papers into the house and dropped
them on the living-room couch. I wasn't ready to face
details yet. The kettle was boiling, so I stepped into the
kitchen and began the morning ritual: empty and rinse the

teapot; warm it with a splash of boiling water; empty the pot again; then add three level teaspoons of Murchie's UVA Highland Ceylon, the strongest tea sold without prescription, guaranteed to unclog synapses and light up middle-aged neurons. I unplugged the kettle, then filled the pot fast while the water was still boiling.

UVA Highland needs four minutes to brew itself into an elixir. I spent the time tapping my fingers on the stainless steel sink, chewing my lip and looking out the window at the blue-white expanse of the Comox glacier, a leftover chunk of the last ice age slumped between two Vancouver Island peaks like a kid's backyard tent made by slinging a sheet over a clothesline. Then I poured a cup and went to where the newspapers were waiting for me.

The biweekly had let the story eat half its front page, but most of that was a long-shot picture of cop cars and the coroner's meat wagon. The RCMP had clapped a lid on the mess until they figured out just exactly what the hell had happened up on the mountain and they weren't telling local journalists anything.

The resulting shortage of facts meant that the Victoria daily could give the story only a few paras on the up-island news page. They were calling it an unexplained explosion. But the *Vancouver Sun* had a bylined piece by the award-winning reporter who covered the city's notorious stock exchange. The Howe Street watchdog had fleshed out the wire-service report with context and background from his own files.

Courtenay RCMP have now identified one of two victims in Tuesday's still unexplained explosion at a Mount Washington construction site as Leonard Geisel, 36, a Vancouver stock promoter.

The identification was made from a wallet and other personal effects found at the scene, said Staff Sergeant Lucien Vaillancourt, head of the local RCMP detachment.

Police now say they have also identified the second victim but are withholding his name.

Geisel was one of a number of VSE operatives recently sought by the Superintendent of Brokers for questioning in an investigation of allegedly illegal trading on the exchange.

Described by sources as a minor fish in some of the VSE's darker backwaters, Geisel was a known associate of promoters suspected of links to organized crime.

He dropped out of sight after taking part in the feeding frenzy last month that surrounded the meteoric rise of shares in White Heart Resources, a junior mining company whose shares were recently ordered frozen by exchange directors "pending clarification of the company's affairs."

He is also believed to have been part of a ring of related companies that inflated the value of penny stocks.

I skimmed the rest of the story. Skirting the rocky coast of outright libel, the reporter conveyed his suspicions. Geisel had probably irritated one of the larger predators that grazed upon the schools of investors lured into the exchange by the bait of get-rich-quick scams. So he had wound up messily dead on Mount Washington. The police had no leads or suspects.

I sipped my tea and read the story through once more, carefully. Then I stretched out on the couch and allowed myself to breathe easily again. There was no indication they'd be coming after me.

It had started only two weeks before, on a Tuesday in late October, when Geisel phoned me. I let the answering machine field the call while I listened in. I'd taken to doing that in case it was the bank manager calling to demand another support payment to maintain my fast-growing overdraft. A month earlier I would have given the Weasel a pass but in September I hadn't known that I was hip deep in a financial swamp and sinking fast.

He was a Howe Street small fry, a hustler who occasionally needed some wordsmithing and would pay for it if you chased him. I had first worked for him three or four years ago, when he wangled the position of editor of a newsletter circulated among alumni of his college fraternity chapter. For a hundred bucks every three months, I ghosted two thousand words of nostalgic rah-rah, and Geisel got to be a good old boy among people he might be able to talk into taking a flutter on the market.

I listened to my own overly cheerful tones coming out of the answering machine — "This is Sid Rafferty. Give me a name and number and I'll call you right back" — then I picked up the hand-set as soon as I heard his frat-rat voice say "Hi guy, got a job for ya … "

"What kind of job?" I asked.

"Brochure, little mining company that's gonna make some noise, next few weeks."

Even though I needed the work — needed it desperately — I also needed to feel superior to the likes of Geisel, even when I was taking his money.

"Jesus, Weasel," I said, "you have no shame."

"Shame? What shame?"

"What we're talking about, it's some chunk of moose pasture. You got a drill rig on it, you're gonna juggle the assay reports and then you wave the punters over the edge of the cliff. Am I right?"

The Weasel did his offended gentleman snort. It was

good. "You are not right. This is clean. Couple guys got this new process … "

"Oh, yeah. Like that couple guys had the satellite imaging technology that was gonna spot the elephants' graveyard." The scam had been a twist on the classic lost treasure con, updated to take account of the international movement to ban the ivory trade. Geisel had netted maybe twenty grand, buying discount stock warrants, using them to scoop up cheap blocks of stock, then feeding them to greedy suckers at rising prices before the bubble burst.

"Yeah, all right, that one, OK … but I'm telling you, Raff, this is no shit. They got the process, some kinda new cyanide leaching thing. It works, man. I got this little cube of platinum right here, they made it themselves."

"Oh, well, why didn't you say? I mean, if you've actually got a cube of platinum, then geez … "

"Look, what is this, you can afford to piss on your friends' money, now you're some big movie writer? You want the job or not?"

I didn't want the job; I needed it, desperately. But I wasn't going to tell him the movie deal was a bust, that I was back to the freelance scrabble after corporate speechwriting, annual reports and any other commercial assignments that would pay my bills. Anytime the Weasel scented blood, his instinct was to bite down hard.

"I'll tell you what I want. I want a cheque for one thousand dollars couriered over here tomorrow and I want another thousand when I hand you the draft. I'll start work when the first cheque clears."

Geisel always made a peculiar noise when people tried to get money out of him. It was a pure tone straight from the unconscious, probably dating back to before he even learned to talk. He'd have made the same plangent bleat, sitting in his highchair, if somebody tried to take his chocolate pudding away. He made it now.

"Whatta you think, I'm the Wizard of Oz," he said, "I'm going to make all your dreams come true? Two grand for a lousy two-fold brochure? Last time was only a thousand."

"It's two grand for a first-class, two-fold brochure. And last time I didn't get paid."

"You got paid."

"I got paid *half*, and that was only because I walked into the Wedgewood dining room, you're having lunch with your wise-guy buddies, you don't want to look like a schmuck being dunned for a bad debt."

"I never paid you the other half?" I could imagine his expression. He'd be wearing his What Red Light, Officer? look.

"Must've slipped your mind. But don't worry, you paid half last time, you pay double this time. It all works out."

"But I just got you the other thing, that's gotta be worth something."

I almost let that one get to me. It was true that Geisel had passed my name to a man who was looking for someone to write a puff piece about a new ski resort on a mountain I could see from my backyard. I was supposed to see the man — Gaspar was his name — this afternoon.

"Listen," I said, "a thing is worth what it's worth. For my quality of work, two grand is a fair price."

The Weasel grumbled — he was good at that too — but he agreed to send the cheque. He'd also send a package of background information on his two inventors, their process and the played-out mine in Montana that they claimed they could bring back into production. I'd craft the copy for a brochure which would pitch a plan to turn the mine into a cornucopia of precious metal, once Geisel and his fellow sharks had accumulated sufficient capital from farsighted investors.

If the "farsighted investors" had been mice their tails would have been in danger from farmers' wives with carving knives, but I put the thought of all those fools with chequebooks out of my mind.

I would do the job for Geisel's two thousand dollars and, yes, I knew what that made me.

There was a time when I'd looked down on the kind of flack who would hire himself out to help a scam artist like the Weasel separate fools from their fortunes. Now that time seemed a long way behind me, back when I'd been a legitimate newsman.

Even then, I was no rising star. I didn't have a journalism degree. I'd dropped out of university at twenty, tired of living on sardines and peanut butter, to take a job in the low-pay ghetto of weekly newspapers. But I could think and I could write, and I'd done both well enough to move first into the newsroom of the *Vancouver Sun* and from there to a spot in the *FP* newspaper syndicate's small Ottawa bureau, where I covered major news and even put out the occasional analytical piece.

Then *FP* had suddenly crashed into oblivion. The Southam chain had scooped up most of the pieces but they already had their own Ottawa bureau. Still, I was not out of work for long. I walked from Parliament Hill across Wellington Street to the National Press Club where the Press Gallery herd was witnessing the demise of a noble newspaper chain by bellowing three deep around the bar. I wasn't even halfway through my first glass of Black Label before the executive assistant to a senior cabinet minister offered me a job as staff speechwriter to his boss.

I said yes, and we clinked glasses. I looked out from the club's third-floor window at the Peace Tower standing serenely above the gothic heaps across the street and I thought, *Raff, that could be a great big opportunity over there.*

I couldn't know that it would turn out to be an opportunity to learn that I wouldn't measure up as a husband, father or just about anything else I'd put my hand to since.

It had taken me ten years to end up flat broke in a beautiful little tourist town on Vancouver Island, hating myself because I had to thank the Weasel for feeding me the only two freelance assignments on my immediate horizon.

Right now I didn't have any more time to hate myself; I had to see the man up on the mountain who wanted fifteen hundred words of adulatory prose about the new Coronado ski resort going in on Mount Washington, just the other side of Courtenay.

The developers had bought a double-page spread in a lifestyle magazine that was dropped free of charge in mailboxes all over Western Canada, providing those mailboxes were attached to houses in upscale neighbourhoods. The wad of cash the developers were putting down for the ad had warmed the magazine editor's tiny heart toward accepting a puff piece lauding the resort's attractions.

The money men would be spending a further $750 to warm my heart; that would be my fee for crafting lines about deep, virgin powder and sophisticated après-ski ambiance. I was a little troubled by not knowing much more about skiing than the fact that yuppies and Norwegians did a lot of it, but I figured I could check out some ski magazines at the library for the feel.

I backed my battered yellow AMC Concord out of the garage through a cloud of blue smoke and headed down the hill to the dike road. The view of the Comox Valley unrolling before me could have been lifted straight from a postcard. Wetlands and farmers' fields flanked the delta where the Puntledge River fed smoothly into the Strait of Georgia's saltchuck. Seals and ducks dunked for food among the reed islands.

Comox is a staging area for migratory birds on the Pacific flyway, and the remnants of transient flocks of Canada geese and trumpeter swans were mooching around the long grass, wrapping up the last items on the bird agenda before heading for the equator.

Across the river the little city of Courtenay ran a grid-work of streets up toward foothills that loggers were scalping with chainsaws and grapple yarders the size of dinosaurs; above the hills, the mountains and the glacier put an interesting edge on the sky.

I sometimes thought that the whole world tilted toward this little coastal valley. Every year flocks of Japanese and German tourists paid thousands to visit for a couple of weeks, to hike in the fossil-laden hills and fish for salmon in the Strait. It seemed as if half the federal folk who ever rotated through CFB Comox air base and the local RCMP detachment came back when they retired. I couldn't blame them. It was a beautiful, quiet place to live, and the prospect of having to move back to the big city was chewing holes in my self-esteem. Which already resembled Swiss cheese.

But unless I lucked into some major new clients pretty soon, I'd be mailing out résumés and trying to worm my way into some forest or mining company's public-relations department. Wearing a suit and tie. Getting to work on time. Saying "yes sir, no sir, three bags full, sir" to some VP for corporate services. Having to smile and kiss ass and pretend that increasing shareholder value was what I lived for.

Or worst of all, having to ask my ex-wife for work.

I crossed the river, worked my way through the old part of Courtenay to Headquarters Road and began the climb toward Mount Washington. Side-by-side city lots gave way to one-hectare parcels, then the trees moved in and I was driving through the second-growth stands of spruce, alder and Douglas fir that line most back roads and highways in British Columbia. After a few kilometres I slowed when I saw a deer browsing beside the road. It was a common sight, but I was still too recently out of the big city not to take a look.

A little farther and the asphalt connected with a logging road, owned and built by the multi-national that held timber rights in this part of Vancouver Island. The road was roughly made, full of switchbacks and steeply graded. If the ski lodge operators wanted the article to mention the approach to their resort, it would be a wordsmith's challenge. I didn't know if I could properly capture the picturesque charm of the sixteen-wheeled behemoth, piled high with logs almost as thick as I was tall, spewing billows of dust and pea gravel, now thundering at me on this deep-ditched, narrow stretch, clearly in the hands of a graduate of the Mad Max school of offensive driving.

I squeezed over to the edge of the road, and the truck swooshed by, close enough to touch if I'd wanted to risk an arm, blinding me with its dust plume. The experience would be even more charming in snow season.

A few minutes later I passed the entrance to the Mount Washington ski resort, the "working man's Whistler" that had opened in the early 1980s and had since steadily attracted skiers who wanted a day on the slopes without doing grievous bodily harm to their credit card balances. From what I knew of the Coronado development, the new resort would draw from a different customer base: the kind of people who believed that spending lots of money on themselves was the fundamental principle upon which the universe was founded.

I kept on going. After ten minutes the winding road rounded a vast pile of stumps and slash, and suddenly there was clear space all around. Several large log-walled and shingle-roofed buildings in various stages of completion clustered around a space at the bottom of a slope that seemed to run kilometres into the sky; it was mostly rock and brown earth now, but even my inexpert eye could see that this place would make skiers' hearts go pitter-pat when the snows came.

Most of the resort was already built. The lodge, a long, low structure with log walls half a metre thick, looked to be ready to stock its restaurants and boutiques. It sprawled across one side of a mud-churned square where construction workers had parked their pickups and four-by-fours; the other sides were occupied by several three-storey blocks of condos with exteriors finished and windows glazed. From inside the nearest, air hammers and some carpenter's boom-box were in a contest to see which could deafen their owners first. Upslope, heavy equipment operators were erecting pylons for the gondola cars that would sweep resort patrons to the top of the mountain in speed and comfort.

My car slewed around in the slick mud, but I managed to stop and park without adding to its extensive collection of dings. I left it next to a gold-on-white Cadillac near the front steps of the lodge, then climbed to the front doors. They were twin slabs of red cedar, skilfully carved in a west coast native motif, balanced to swing open at a baby's touch.

I wiped my shoes on a drop-sheet that lay across the doorstep and went inside. The lobby was big but it might look smaller once they added furniture, carpeting and guests in thousand-dollar ski suits. My first impression was that all the trees they'd stripped off the slopes to make ski runs had been debarked, varnished and stacked up like a kid's building set. There was more cedar, polished and grainy, in every direction except up, where the log walls rose to support a segmented steel-and-glass dome. The flood of daylight left no corner in darkness. This was a place for people who wanted to be seen.

The lobby was empty. I did the natural thing: I went to the front desk and looked for a bell to ring. They hadn't provided it yet, but I noticed that one end of the counter top was hinged and open like a drawbridge. I pushed aside the gate underneath and stepped behind the desk. A frosted glass door in the panelled wall said "PRIVATE"; behind it was a narrow hallway between offices with closed doors. I heard indistinct voices down the hall and followed them.

At the end of the passage I turned a corner and bumped into something big in a shiny suit, something that had apparently just climbed out of a vat of Blue Stratos cologne. I bounced off and coughed. He was taller than me and a lot wider, with a beef-fed mid-thirties face, curly black hair and an overdeveloped taste for gold jewellery. We hadn't met, but already I could tell we were never going to be friends.

"Whattaya want? We ain't open," he said.

"I'm here to see a Mr. Gaspar."

"Yeah? What for?"

"He's hiring me to write a magazine piece about this place."

He grunted, turned around and walked into an office. A moment passed and then he stuck his head out and looked at me, flat-eyed. "You want me to fuckin' carry you?"

I followed him through the door into what would someday be the hotel manager's office. Right now it contained only a battered steel desk covered in blueprints, three-ring binders and a computer, and two chairs on castors. One of the chairs creaked as Blue Stratos sat down, crossed his legs and stared out the window. The other was occupied by a small man who reminded me of the fetal animal cadavers they used to make us cut up for grade eleven biology. He was pink, wrinkled and mostly hairless, looking up from the computer screen and blinking at me as I put on my cheerful PR consultant persona and stuck out a hand.

"Mr. Gaspar?" I asked. When he half rose and extended a cold, pale hand, I grabbed it, pumped it and didn't let go of it until I'd told him who I was and what I was there for. According to the books I'd read, this was a surefire way to assure clients of my unalloyed confidence that I'd do an excellent job for them.

The confidence is supposed to be contagious, but life had immunized Gaspar. He got his hand back as soon as he could and put his eyes everywhere except on me, his head ducked between his shoulders like a dog waiting for a swat from a rolled-up newspaper.

"Please sit down," he said, then realized that the only other seat was taken. Blue Stratos showed no inclination to vacate it. He had slowly rotated the chair to face me and was now leaning back in it, giving me a look you'd remember if you'd ever been a teenager going to dances at some East Vancouver community centre or strip-mall disco. Out on the dance floor would be the kids who came to bop, but hanging around the fire doors were the guys who came to fight. They always gave you the look: head back, lazy-eyed, mouth open a little.

I hadn't been on the receiving end of the look in maybe twenty years but now I was feeling the tightening shiver in the back muscles, the neck hairs lifting, the coolness of skin that says, *Adrenalin on line, here we go.* Meanwhile I was thinking *This is nuts* and meeting his look with as neutral and unchallenging a gaze as I could manage. None of the books advised aspiring public-relations practitioners to get into adolescent ball-weighing contests with clients at the first encounter.

"Lou," said Gaspar. "Would you give us a few minutes? Please?"

Lou slid his eyes from me to Gaspar and back again, so slowly I just knew he'd practised it in mirrors. Then just as slowly he looked away, eased out of the chair and left the office. A lot of his cologne decided to hang around.

I sat down. Gaspar looked like a kid caught doing something he was too old for. It struck me that neither of these two meshed with my preconceptions about developers of multi-million dollar properties. I had considerable faith in my preconceptions, because I'd met some of the money men who had remade downtown Vancouver during the development boom of the eighties. But I didn't have to wonder long about why Gaspar didn't fit the pattern. It was because, like me, he was hired help.

He told me he was a certified general accountant who had signed on as controller and project manager for the limited partnership that was turning this mountainside into a money-making machine. The side of beef I'd collided with in the hall was Lou Savelek, whom Gaspar described as "in charge of shareholder liaison."

I was beginning to see that the Coronado resort did not fit the usual pattern: development by a small core of experts underwritten by the investments of cash-fat doctors and dentists, with everybody either doubling their money in five years or writing off a tax loss. If that had been the case, a couple of those savvy hustlers would be on-site. Since there was nobody here but a salaried bean counter and his no-neck babysitter, it began to look as if the money behind all this came from the kind of people who never planned for tax losses because they never paid taxes.

Not that it mattered to me either way. I'd done a job or two for companies whose principals seemed a little out of the ordinary, but their money had been as good as anybody else's, and I'd always been paid. So I mentally filed my speculations about Coronado's backers under the heading of Who Cares? and paid attention to what Gaspar was telling me.

He gave me a quick overview of the development itself and a copy of an informal prospectus that must have been originally prepared for a very small readership, probably three guys in the back room of a pool hall on Commercial Drive. But it was succinctly put together and contained all the hard information I needed on the number and types of condo units, services and amenities at the lodge, speed and capacity of the gondola lift and so on. I skimmed the document, asked a few questions and in ten minutes I was fully loaded with facts. Now it was time to go out and soak up some atmosphere.

Lou was in the Cadillac, playing a CD loud with the windows rolled up. It sounded familiar, maybe something from the Beach Boys' car-culture period. I decided not to find out.

Growing up in the succession of blue-collar neighbourhoods through which my family had wandered, I'd learned early that my best hope for dealing with the look from a Lou Savelek was to talk my way out of it. I'd never been a great fighter, so I had become a great talker, able to generate a plausible spiel — or at least a dense fog of bullshit — that often enough left bullies and tough guys shaking their heads while I backed safely out of range. It was no wonder I'd turned out to be a pretty good speechwriter; I'd trained in a hard school.

I headed for the nearest low-rise condo across the mud patch. The building's exterior was more cedar. As far as I could see, the logs looked neatly joined and finished. Another set of carved doors, smaller than those at the main lodge, then yet more cedar, including a staircase that rose from the foyer and circled the walls up to the third floor.

I climbed to the first landing, pushed through a glass fire door and entered a hallway that could have been in a good hotel anywhere in the world, except for the wires dangling from the ceiling and the doors to the suites leaning against the walls like tired dominoes.

I checked out a suite and found it spacious, the carpets laid, fixtures all in place, including a Jacuzzi-for-two handy to the bedroom. The view would be worth paying for, once it was covered in snow. Add some plush furniture, pipe gas into the glass-doored fireplace, and this place would justify my using words like "sumptuous" and "luxurious" in the article I'd be writing.

I climbed to the top floor. The units here were definitely first-class, although the gold-on-black bathroom was probably more Lou's taste than my own. Through the floor-to-ceiling window in a sitting room, I saw him squeeze out of the Cadillac and saunter back to the lodge. I didn't figure him for a skier: bowling, maybe, or bocce. Most likely his favourite form of exercise involved some poor bastard's knee and elbow joints and a ball-peen hammer.

But the more I looked around Coronado, the more Lou Savelek's presence made sense. Somebody was spreading a thick layer of money over this piece of mountain and that somebody wanted a watchdog for his investment. The mob believes in managing for minimal risk.

Fifteen minutes later I'd seen all the interiors I needed to see and was taking a look at the gondola lift's base station. Built of fieldstone, raw beams and plate glass, it was big enough to hold a car that would in turn hold twenty skiers. The big wheel and its massive diesel engine were installed but they wouldn't be pulling the cable into place until the upslope towers were ready.

I stepped outside and jotted down a few words in my notebook: "smooth, silent ride" and "rapid turnaround." I looked up, figuring I'd gathered all the information I'd need. Then I noticed a small building a little way downhill, not much more than a steel hut surrounded by a chain-link fence and set back among the trees. Pump house, I thought. There was a sign on the fence, black on yellow, but too distant to make out the lettering.

I wandered over to see what it said. After stumbling across three sets of bulldozer tracks gouged in the future ski slope, I could read the big word at the top of the sign and the slightly smaller one below. The big one read "DANGER"; the little one was "EXPLOSIVES." Stump blasting, I thought.

"Can I help you?" said a voice behind me.

I turned around. He was a few years younger, just pushing thirty. The hardhat, clipboard and iron ring on the little finger of one hand said "engineer." The expression said he was suspicious of people wandering around where he was working.

I gave him the same handshake and introduction I'd given Gaspar, and he loosened up a little. He told me his name was Mark Betchley and he was a consultant from a company called Alpine Systems. He had laid out the ski runs that led down to Coronado.

I told him it looked pretty good to me and asked him how he thought it ranked against some of the other ski developments on the coast.

"This is as good as it gets," he said.

We talked a little more, and I began to realize that Betchley's feelings about skiing approximated those of the average medieval saint about prayer. In laying out the

Coronado runs, he was building his equivalent of Chartres Cathedral.

"It's the finest work I've ever done, that I've ever been allowed to do," he said. "Can't say enough about the people behind this development. Other jobs, the money's always looking to cut corners. You know, if there's a way to do it 10 percent cheaper, that's the way they want it, even if it's 50 percent worse. But these guys, they just say get it done right. It's great."

This sounded promising. I began to weigh the chances of inflating the puff piece fee to the thousand-dollar mark. My attention was wandering, anyway, as Betchley launched into a lecture on slope stability and average rates of descent. As he talked, we drifted downhill toward the fenced-in steel hut.

By the time we got there, I'd heard my fill about ski runs. When he took a breath, I tapped the warning sign and said, "What do we have here?"

Betchley shrugged. "Avalanche control."

That might be interesting. I flipped over a new page in my notebook. "What do you do, drop dynamite into the snowdrifts?"

"No. We use artillery."

He fished out a ring of keys, selected one and opened the padlock on the gate. Another key worked the lock on the shed door and he opened it wide. Inside, against one wall, was a stack of waxed cardboard boxes, drab green with black lettering stencilled on the side. But most of the shed was taken up by a battered wooden trailer with rubber tires, like something a farmer might hitch to his tractor for hauling rocks out of a field.

The bed of the trailer supported a framework of tubular steel in which was cradled what I first took to be a length of stovepipe painted olive drab. Then I noticed that the near end of the pipe was capped by a massive cylinder of metal with slits cut into its sides and a handle that curved out and around like an old-fashioned gearshift topped with a ball of polished steel.

I peered at the contraption. "What is this, some kind of CO_2 cannon?"

"What, you mean like compressed air? Hell, no. This is your basic 105-millimetre recoilless anti-tank rifle. Korean War vintage, probably."

"Anti-tank rifle? You mean like a cannon?"

He stepped inside the shed and rubbed his hand on the ball grip. "Yeah, like a cannon, except it's made to be mounted on a jeep or a truck, I guess. Only weighs about four hundred kilos. But it fires an armour-piercing round that would go right through the old-time tanks, maybe even a modern one, for all I know."

"What the hell are you doing with an anti-tank gun at a ski resort?"

"Ah, they use these all over." He pushed the lever, and the thick end of the pipe swung open to reveal a ten-centimetre hole. Betchley stooped and blew imaginary dust from the shiny smooth interior. "The highways department's got a couple dozen in places where there's regular danger of avalanches. Mostly they're in fixed positions, set in concrete and steel, wherever there's a risk of avalanche knocking out main roads in the mountains. But they've got a few that are rigged like this on trailers so they can go where they're needed."

He slammed the breech closed and fondled the thick plug of steel. His eyes lost focus for a moment. "These things really do a job. You can get off three rounds in twenty seconds, easy. Fump, fump, fump! Wham, wham, wham! And then, whoa, about a million tonnes of snow comes rolling and sliding down the hill, snapping off trees, making the weirdest sound you ever ... " He came back to earth, looked a little abashed. "Well, you know what I mean."

I didn't but I said I did. It can be embarrassing when a grown man suddenly turns into a little kid, unless it happens during some football-or-hockey-game-beer-drenched-male-bonding situation. I patted the cannon's breech, and for lack of anything else to say, asked him how it worked.

I should have been warned by the mini-course on ski runs: Mark Betchley was one of those frustrated lecturers who are always primed to let go. He carried a fair burden of knowledge about recoilless rifles and he unloaded a lot of it on me over the next five minutes, while I nodded and made polite noises.

I learned that avalanche control meant firing a standard military round — whether of the armour-piercing variety or the shrapnel variety depended on abstruse snow conditions — into the right part of a snowpack at the right time. The twenty-kilo cartridge was mostly propellant in a cardboard tube attached to the warhead. You slipped it into the breech, closed up, sighted through the side-mounted telescopic sight and fired.

It had a five-kilometre range and, of course, no recoil. Having fired a .22 as a kid, I didn't see how a round as long as my arm wouldn't kick back, but Betchley showed me the slits on the sides of the breech and told me they were exhaust ports for explosive gases recaptured in the barrel. You could stand right behind the breech block when the gun fired and you'd be fine. But if you were standing beside one of the exhaust ports, the blast of gases from the slits would rip the flesh from your bones.

It didn't look up to the job, but I took his word for it that, in the right hands, this tube on a toy trailer could kill a tank or blow a bunker to smithereens. Which led me to speculate how, in the wrong hands, this piece of ordnance might do the same thing to an armoured car or a bank vault.

He shook his head. "Nah. Well, maybe if you were going for gold bullion. But if you wanted paper money or stock certificates, all you'd end up with would be fly ash. This is no neutron bomb. It doesn't take out the people and leave everything else intact."

He patted one of the boxes stacked against the wall. "This is an armour-piercing round," he said. "Know how it works?"

I shook my head.

"There's a shaped charge in here: explosive in the shape of a hollow cone. It goes off when it hits something hard like a tank. The explosion shoots a jet of superheated high-density metal that instantly melts through the armour. It's like hitting a pat of butter with a stream of boiling water. Anything that's burnable inside the tank — ammunition, fuel, people's clothes, the people in them — it burns.

"Now, an armoured car, that's like a tank full of paper." He lowered the anti-tank round into its box and replaced the lid. "Using one of these would be like giving the inside of the truck a quick squirt from a blast furnace. Shrapnel round would just bounce off. Although it would give anybody inside a first-class headache."

We went back out into the sunshine. I thanked him and put away my notebook. Five minutes later I was raising dust along the logging road, heading back to Comox. I started thinking about the cannon and how it might figure as a plot device in a movie script. Maybe some dim-witted Dillinger wannabes steal a recoilless rifle to knock over a bank but in the end all they have are charred bank notes.

That was as far as I got before another monster logging truck rolled up behind me and used its air horn to lift the hair on the back of my neck. I spent the next fifteen minutes trying to keep it from eating the Concord's rear end.

Besides, I'd blown it in the movie-writing business.

Two

TRUTH MAY BE STRANGER than fiction, but you don't get to do any rewrites.

My brief career as a screenwriter could have been one of those high-concept scripts that agents can summarize in ten words or less: unknown gets break, soars high, crash lands in cow pie.

During one of the intermittent periods when business was good, I had generated enough cash to justify renting a small office among the big towers in downtown Vancouver. The landlord was an outfit that provided executive services — mail, telephone answering, reception and secretarial help — for a monthly fee. One of my neighbours ran the west-coast office of Telefilm Canada, the federal agency that financed movies and TV pilots. Before long I was writing reader's reports on scripts being considered for funding. Along the way I learned a thing or two about the movie business.

One day my friend the fed came across the hall and dropped a newspaper clipping on my desk. "Why not try this?" she said.

The clipping was from *Cinema Canada,* a movie trade paper. A Toronto-based pay-TV service needed story ideas for a murder mystery that could be used in a promotional contest: the movie would air on pay-TV a few times without the ending; viewers could write in and say whodunit and why. The first correct entry would win a trip.

I was not a devotee of murder mysteries but I thought I knew the recipe. Take one corpse, mix in a handful of plausible suspects, sprinkle with clues and red herrings, whip up some suspense and garnish with a quirky detective who figures it all out. The rest is mainly setting and character.

"This is not really my kind of thing," I said.

"You could give it a shot," she said.

I wasn't going to take her advice. But as I drove home through afternoon traffic, I got to thinking about murder and mayhem. It seemed to me that the key was the setting. It needed a setting and some characters that would be original and have audience appeal. Halfway home I hit on the pop music industry. By the time I reached my rented pile of carpenter's gothic in quiet south Vancouver, the principal characters were talking together in my head.

I sat in the kitchen with pen and notepad, and they all poured out fully formed as if they'd been wandering around inside me for years looking for the exit. I stopped to warm up last night's spaghetti, but they kept pulling me back to the paper, the way my twin boys used to when they wanted to show me something they'd built under the porch.

The spaghetti burned while I plotted out the buildup to the first murder, but I ate it anyway, taking bites while jotting down snatches of dialogue and character details. When it was all done and tied together, I was still too buzzed to let go. I clicked on the TV and watched fifteen different programs in three minutes. Finally I gave up, grabbed the pages of notes and went back downtown.

The other tenants on my floor had gone home; the only sound was the shush of the air recycling system. I flipped the switch on my ancient twin-drive, third-hand Superbrain — its video board apparently soldered by distracted monkeys — and started punching the keys.

Around midnight I stepped into the rain on West Georgia Street. In my pocket was a diskette holding in its vinyl memory a three-page story outline about a lesbian rhythm-and-blues legend, a country star with a long-forgotten rap sheet, a lethal erotomaniac and a low-key police detective who listened to nothing but Mozart and Brahms.

Now that I'd got them out of my head, I could go home and sleep.

The next morning I polished the outline, ran it through

the C. Itoh daisy wheel — which printed with a noise like Cossacks machine-gunning peasants from a slow-moving train — then headed over to see Roger Gambowsky.

Roger was an ex-CBC writer-director-producer who had escaped to make corporate videos and — he hoped — feature films. I'd written some video scripts for him. He was honest and I liked him.

He had an office in a turn-of-the-century building a five-minute walk from the Howe Street financial district, near the art school and Catholic cathedral. He got his space free from some hard-shelled stock-market operators who were backing his stab at video production.

Three or four of these Howe Street middleweights spent their afternoons in a rear office, playing a variation of rummy they called Nanaimo. I sat in once while waiting for Roger to get back from a meeting and lost sixty bucks just learning the rules.

Roger read my story outline and the trade paper clipping. "Jeez," he said. "It's not worth my time, Raff. Two hundred people are going to send in submissions. It's a goddamn lottery."

"I'm sending it," I said. "I think it's better coming from a producer, but if you don't want to do it, I'll send it myself."

He shrugged, and we made a deal. He would send the story to the pay-TV people in Toronto. If they bought it, he would produce the movie, I would get a sixty grand fee and we would split the producer's net fifty-fifty. He drew up a simple contract; I read it and signed. Then we waited.

About a month later Roger phoned. "You're not going to believe this."

"I'm known for my gullibility," I said. "Try me."

"I just got off the phone with Toronto." He paused, and I knew he was shaking his head. "We got us a development deal."

"Meaning?"

"Meaning they want a twenty-page treatment. If they like it, they'll put up money for a draft script."

"What kind of money?"

"Two grand for the treatment, eight for the draft."

My god, I thought, but what I said was, "That's not Writer's Guild or ACTRA scale." I'd read everything I could on what writers charged for screenwriting.

I could sense that Roger was shaking his head again. "A lot of writers are assholes," he said, "but it's not an actual prerequisite."

I kept my mouth shut.

"First," he continued, "you're not being hired to write a script. You're a coproducer who's being offered a development fee to launch the project — a fee which goes right into your pocket. Second, this is a *major* break. There are writers who would saw off sensitive body parts for a chance to do this script on spec, whereas you are getting ten grand, rain or shine."

"You're right," I said.

"I love it when you say that."

"Call them back. Tell 'em we'll take the deal."

"Ah, I'll wait a couple of days," he said. "Why should writers have all the fun?"

From there on in, it just kept clicking into place. Toronto loved the treatment. Within a month, I had a cheque for two thousand dollars and was turning out a screenplay. It was the most fun I'd ever had sitting down.

Old clients called me; I put them off, said try this writer I'd worked with or that one I'd heard about. I turned down work and turned off some regular customers. I could smell the bridges burning but I didn't much care.

Roger was doing producer things. First he tapped his investors for seed money. Then he got the CBC to agree to broadcast the movie after its pay-TV showing; that made us eligible for federal funding. Then he dealt in a distributor who would put us into the video end-market.

Everything went smoothly, to Roger's disbelief. "This doesn't happen," he would tell me. "Making movies is heartbreak and disappointment. You don't walk in first time and get it handed to you."

"God likes writers," I told him. "In the Bible, Jesus is always hanging out with his biographers."

But I was thinking, *Maybe this time I'm actually going to make it.*

The production budget totalled $1.6 million. With everybody on board — pay-TV, broadcast network, the feds, Roger's Nanaimo-playing backers and the video distributor — we now had commitments for $1.35 million. Roger booked a flight to L.A. He had an appointment to see a man called Erlenmeyer, a veep with an American pay-TV company. I drove him to the airport and we had a drink in the lounge overlooking the parked wide-bodies.

"Erlenmeyer's the key. If we get him," he said, "we'll have the quarter mil to fill the budget."

Then Roger would gather all the money into one place, and we would make a movie. But if we did not get a deal in the next few weeks, all the other commitments would lapse and the money would walk on to other projects.

"Try for a headlock," I advised Roger. "Cut off his air supply until he signs a deal."

"Where'd you learn your negotiating skills?" he asked.

"My ex-wife's lawyer."

Roger came back a couple of days later with his fingers crossed. Erlenmeyer was pitching us to his boss.

In the meantime I finished the first draft script and sent it to Toronto. They asked for minor changes; I made them, and back came a cheque for eight thousand — I kissed it, then cashed it. Roger couriered the new script to Erlenmeyer. We waited some more.

We were in Roger's office, working on a video to promote a helicopter shuttle between downtown Vancouver and the provincial capital, Victoria, when the fax gurgled. Roger stooped over the machine to read the sheet as it stuttered out of the slot.

"It's L.A.," he said. "They're in. We are go. Erlenmeyer's sending up a contract next week. I don't believe this."

The papers were lawyered by one of Roger's backers. Cheques were cut and deposited in a trust fund. Roger, with a cellular phone grafted to his ear, was talking to agents and union reps, lining up a cast and crew.

"What should I do?" I asked him.

"Go away," he said.

"No, really," I said.

"Yes, really." He asked somebody to hold for a moment. "Your part is wrapped. There will be rewrites, and I'll call you in. Right now there's nothing here but the nasty, messy part of movie-making. Which I take care of. When we start to shoot, you come in and I'll give you sixty K plus maybe a folding chair with your name on it. But for now, why don't you go write another movie?"

"Oh," I said, never at a loss for words.

"In fact," he said, pulling a file folder out of his desk, "why don't you go and write this one?"

It was a movie-of-the-week he had outlined and filed away long ago. The folder contained a plot summary, main character sketches and the first twenty pages of a draft script. It was about dysfunctional families with a Romeo and Juliet twist. And he had lined up some development funding from my friend at the federal film agency.

"It's not a big fee — seven grand," he said. "But it's a nice little story. I was going to do it, but hey, who's got the time, right?"

I took the folder, drove home and found a battered pick-up parked in front of the house. The sign on the door said "DHALIWAL BROTHERS DECONSTRUCTION," and two guys in work clothes and turbans were giving the place the once-over.

"Looking to buy?" I asked them. The landlord had told me he was thinking of selling when he'd last slid in from Santa Barbara, where he conveniently didn't have to talk to Revenue Canada. He did appear regularly on my TV, however, in an infomercial that starred a guy who told you how to get rich in real estate by picking the bones of recent widows and divorcing couples — "motivated sellers" was how he described them. My landlord gazed solemnly into the camera and opined that one could become a winner just by thinking like a winner. He mentioned Daniel in the lions' den.

"This place is sold," said the larger of the Dhaliwals.

"It's coming down. The buyers are going to build two new houses."

"Double lot," said the smaller one.

"Nobody told me anything," I said.

"They don't speak much English. They'll probably let their lawyer do the talking."

The new owners were polite but they wanted me out fast. Their lawyer even offered me a thousand dollars if I would leave in one month instead of the three I could legally stay for. I took the grand, added it to what I'd got from the pay-TV people and made a down payment on a hillside house in Comox. It was where I'd always wanted to live, ever since I'd visited local Liberals on some long-ago trip with the justice minister — a place where prices were reasonable and where a guy could probably write some nice movies.

I took my old landlord's advice and dared to be a Daniel. I bought a good computer with circuits that had been soldered by dependable Japanese robots. I added a laser printer and a fax machine and sat down to be up and coming. Over the next few weeks I gazed at the view, walked on the beach and did all the other things done by sensitive writers in coffee commercials.

I also finished the first draft of Roger's dysfunctional families script and sent it to him.

"Looks good," he said when he phoned after reading it. "Downshifting must agree with you."

"What's downshifting?"

"What you're doing," he said. "Moving out of the city, trading the big-money rat race for small-town peace and quiet. Kicking back."

"OK," I said, "I'm a downshifter. I'll go out and look at a sunset or something."

He called a few days later. I was sitting on the sundeck, watching a vee of trumpeter swans flap their way up from the river flats. It was a perfect day. For the first time in a lot of years I was feeling genuinely good about myself, as if maybe the long and steady rain had stopped, and I was going to see some sunlight pouring in at last. I was thinking about how nice it would be to have the twins over, how I could show them a good time.

"You're right," I told Roger as soon as I recognized his voice. "I'm a downshifter extraordinaire."

"You're not going to believe this," he said.

"You always say that."

"Erlenmeyer. He's dead. Heart attack."

"Ah, too bad." The sun was putting a frame of Jacob's ladders around the Comox glacier. I wished I was a painter so that I could try to capture the precise shade of purple that lay between the peaks.

"No, not too bad. Try total fucking disaster," said Roger.

"What?"

"Erlenmeyer was our shepherd on the pay-TV project. Now that he's taken Type A retirement, some guy called Gresham is sitting in Erlenmeyer's office and he's making noises like he's got better things to do."

The sundeck didn't seem so warm now. "Roger, what are you saying?"

"I'm saying it looks like it's unravelling." I knew he would be shaking his head. "We're going to lose it, Raff."

There was now a definite chill in the air. "But they signed a contract. Tell the bastards we'll sue 'em."

He gave a tired laugh. "Sure, all we need is an L.A. law firm and a thirty thousand dollar retainer."

"Ah, Christ," I said.

"It gets worse," he said.

A shiver walked up from my tailbone to my neck and settled there like a cold wet hand. "Tell me."

"The Romeo and Juliet thing is sinking too. Ottawa's cutting back on movie financings. They'll probably give us the seven for the script but no follow-up funding. And," he sighed, and I tensed, "most of that seven grand is going to have to be applied to costs on the pay-TV deal. My backers are out some up-front money and they aren't going to let that cash just flow through the company books."

"I need that money to live on, Roger," I said. "I've been counting on that and the sixty thousand from pay-TV. My banker's already bugging me about the overdraft."

"Sorry, Raff. Look, I'll make sure you get at least a couple of thou, but hey … "

"Yeah, hey." Something bad was creeping around in my gut.

"I'll let you know what happens."

He hung up. The swans were gone, the clouds had foreclosed on the Jacob's ladders and the mountains were just big cold hunks of hard rock.

The day after I toured Coronado I went down to the Comox branch of the Vancouver Island Regional Library and spent a couple of hours going through ski magazines to get the feel for the puff piece. When I got back there was a message on the machine to call the bank.

I ate a little canned soup, then cranked up the computer and bashed out the ski piece in one sustained burst of nervous energy. When I pushed the function key to save the draft, I checked the clock and told myself that any self-respecting bank-branch manager would have gone home by 4:55, so I could put off calling him until tomorrow.

At 7:55 the next morning a Loomis courier banged on the door. I was already up and waiting for him. I signed for Geisel's thousand-dollar cashier's cheque and a package of bumf on how to use the cyanide-leaching process to extract precious minerals from thinly disseminated ore bodies. I didn't have time to read it.

By 8:10 I had slipped the cashier's cheque into the night deposit box at the bank, along with a note telling the manager I was called over to Vancouver by a client and would talk to him when I got back. I had parked on the side of the bank away from his office window and crept around the corner like a guy making a midnight withdrawal.

I cut over to the Payless gas station, where they still hadn't installed an electronic approval system for credit card purchases, and tanked up the Concord. I talked the attendant into adding fifty in cash to the gas receipt, which gave me ferry fare to Vancouver and back. The sun came out, and I headed south for the long drive to the B.C. Ferries Corporation terminal at Nanaimo.

If I were doing a tourist brochure for upper Vancouver Island, I would say that Highway 17 meanders, at a pace reminiscent of bygone days, along the coast between tranquil evergreen forests and the rolling breakers of Georgia Strait.

If I were writing a speech for the opposition's highway critic in the provincial legislative assembly, I would call it a dangerous two-lane goat trail with too many tourists pushing Winnebagos and pulling boats. The visitors' leisurely pace frustrates the local four-by-four jockeys into passing on blind curves, leaving the cry of "asshole!" drifting back on the summer air.

But in late October the traffic's not too bad, so I made it to Nanaimo in time to roll up the ramp onto the 11 a.m. sailing. I put the Concord where the man waved me to stop behind the semi-trailers in the ferry's cavernous lower deck. I went up the companionway, straight through the passenger areas and out onto the deck. The boat's diesels roared and kicked hell out of the water astern. She trembled against the dock like an insecure whale getting up the courage to leave home, then surged smoothly across Departure Bay and out into the Strait.

Gulls hovered over our wake while flights of cormorants arrowed across our course, the tips of their black wings almost tickling the wave tops. I walked to the bow, getting an argument from the wind until I forced my way around the wings of the bridge and reached the relatively still air in the centre of the bow. I leaned on the rail to watch as the boat rounded tiny, barren Snake Island, passed the mouth of the bay and struck out for Vancouver.

Over on the mainland the morning's last clouds had pulled back to mooch around the peaks of the Coastal Range, leaving nothing but sea and sunlit sky, green islands and half-timbered mountains, with the towers of downtown Vancouver beginning to show white through the haze to the east. I could see why German burghers and Japanese salarymen loved this place. And I swore for the umpteenth time that I would do whatever was necessary to keep on living where I was living.

With the movie deal dead and some of my best former clients not taking my calls, I was going to have to scramble again for nickel-dime writing jobs. That didn't bother me; I'd gotten used to living off the avails of prostituting the promising writing talent I'd once had. But I'd built up the Comox Valley to my boys, made it out to be one big summer camp, with kayaking and horseback trips and all the rest of the fun stuff that had prompted the local Chamber of Commerce to label the place the world's recreation capital.

I knew Bill and Dick were really looking forward to spending some time with me when school let out. But unless I could somehow get back into earning a reliable income, the only activity I could offer the kids would be an educational day in line at the food bank. The last thing I wanted to do was to move back to Vancouver, rent another dump and invite the kids to hang around the backyard.

I jumped like a tourist when the ferry's whistle blasted to warn off a couple of pleasure craft outside the harbour. I let the wind blow me back around the corner of the bridge and went into the boat's forward lounge, where I found a copy of the Victoria *Times-Colonist* in a recycling bin and caught up on what the world had been doing to itself since the last time I looked.

The lead story told about the hordes of East Germans who were swarming through Hungary into Austria, crammed into smoky little Trabant cars whose technological sophistication made Yugos look like Ferraris.

At home the provincial government was musing about stocking South African wines in the government-run liquor stores again — the latest flaky idea from the increasingly flaky Vander Zalm administration. I wondered if I should go banging on cabinet ministers' doors down at the Legislature, where I used to get the occasional speechwriting assignment back when Bill Bennett was premier. But even if I could stomach crafting glib phrases for the bozo-ocracy that was now running the province, I'd have to move to Victoria. That was only slightly less worse than chasing corporate dollars in the big city.

Two hours later the Concord was a yellow corpuscle in the stream of traffic flowing over the Lions Gate Bridge and through Stanley Park into downtown Vancouver. I barrelled up Georgia to Howe Street, eased between jaywalkers to turn the corner and dropped down the underground parking-garage ramp into Pacific Centre.

The elevator took me up to the lower shopping concourse, and a two-minute weave through shoppers and teenage mall rats led to the internal entrance to the lobby of the Stock Exchange Tower. It was like passing through an invisible curtain: on one side the mall crowd streamed among the stores in anything from grunge to drop-dead chic; on the other the tower lobby was all pinstripes and herringbone tweed, punctuated by couriers dressed like extras in a movie about twenty-first century Italian biker gangs.

I crowded into an elevator with a flock of suits and got off at the twelfth floor. The hall was done in beige and cream, the doors in solid wood with brass lettering beside each office. I crossed to the one marked "GEISEL, CHELMSFORD — BROKERS" and went in.

The place was small, the furniture and the art on the walls the kind you buy at factory outlets. Geisel's space was in the back, a half-glassed office behind a closed door with a plaque that showed his name in black on silver. There was no office for Chelmsford because he didn't exist; Geisel had added the name because he thought it gave his outfit a WASPy, old-money feel.

The receptionist was out for lunch or a pee, or maybe just to get a few minutes' relief from the sound of Geisel bleating into the phone. I couldn't make out the words, but his tone said eloquently that somebody was giving the Weasel a bad time, somebody he couldn't invite to plant a big wet one on his bepimpled butt.

I waited until he hung up, then opened his door and stepped in. He was staring at the cellular phone on his desk. He turned his head and gave me the show of teeth that he thought was a smile, but underneath it I could see that something had the Weasel thoroughly rattled.

"Something wrong?" I asked.

He stretched the grimace a little wider. "Nah. Piece of cake."

I didn't press him; I didn't really care.

He rearranged some papers on his desk and waved me toward a chair. "You got the cheque?" he said.

I sat down. "I'm here, aren't I?" I said.

"Did you read the stuff?"

I nodded. I'd read the mishmash of background material on the ferry. There were excerpts from the prospectus Geisel had filed with the Securities Commission on behalf of High Country Mining Ltd., a new company whose stock would be listed on the VSE once the exchange's governors approved it. There were a couple of articles from a U.S. mining journal about chemically recovering precious metals from the tailings piles of played-out mines and a *Newsweek* piece about strategic minerals. There were sample brochures from other mining plays.

And there were three pages of handwritten technical notes and jottings I couldn't begin to decipher. They looked to have been ripped out of a lab book, then folded and refolded and carried around in somebody's hip pocket long enough for the creases to set.

I opened my note pad and got my pen ready. "What kind of copy are you looking for?"

"Standard pitch but low-key," he said. "Don't promise

'em the moon. But when this thing gets rolling, some people are going to give it a push, and we should see a pretty good climb."

"What aspect do you want me to concentrate on?"

He shrugged again. "I guess the nub is these two guys with the leaching thing. You know how cyanide leaching works?"

I did. I'd written community-relations copy for a mining project in the San Bernardino Mountains. A Canadian company had revived a gold mine abandoned at the turn of the century after primitive mining methods had dug out the richest ores.

The modern miners targeted the low-grade ore around the played out seams. They scooped out tonnes of rock, crushed it to the size of pebbles, then piled it up in vast heaps like pyramids with the top third sliced away. Then they dripped a solution of sodium cyanide on top of the pile; as it seeped down through the ore it dissolved out minute particles of gold. The mineral-heavy solution was caught by a plastic layer under the heap and piped to an extraction process. It left the mine as doré bars of unrefined gold.

"These guys of yours, the scientists, they're supposed to have come up with a better process that will let them mine even lower-grade ore, right?"

"That's what they tell me."

"It's a little hard to believe," I said. The San Bernardino outfit had been processing ore at only about one gram of gold per tonne of rock. Much lower than that, it costs more to mine it than you can sell it for. You lose money on every shovelful. That's why there were virtually no platinum mines in North America, even though the stuff was more valuable than gold.

He gave me his deadpan stare. "You cash the cheque?"

"Yeah."

"So what more convincing do you need?"

I shrugged.

"Look, what do you want me to tell you?" He leaned back in his swivel chair. As far as he knew, these were legit mining guys. They had degrees. They had certificates from Montana Tech, the most prestigious mining-engineering school on the continent, and the University of Witwatersrand. They'd consulted on big projects in Australia, South Africa, the Northwest Territories. "They come in here with a little cube of platinum, tell me they made it in their lab out of a couple barrels of ore shipped up from Butte or somewhere. They show me numbers and give me a lot of yadda-yadda. Are they blowing smoke up my ass? I'm supposed to care? I don't care, I can sell them either way. You wanna know if they're for real, go ask them."

"Give me an address."

He scribbled on a pad, tore off the sheet and handed it to me. "They're there this afternoon. I just talked to them. I'll call, say you're coming."

"Tell them I'll be a couple of hours. I want to read up on this stuff a little more before I go."

"Whatever," he said. His cellular rang, and he answered it with a dignified. "Geisel, Chelmsford." He listened for ten seconds, and I saw the colour fade out of his face like an old Polaroid left in the sun. He sat up and hunched over the phone.

"Where'd you hear this?" he said into the phone and listened. "Well, check it out for Chrissake and get back to me!" He punched the off button and let the phone slip into his lap, stared at his polished wingtips. He'd already forgotten I was there.

After a few seconds I cleared my throat. He looked up, startled. I'd never seen a more worried look on the Weasel's face.

"I got nothing more to tell you," he said. "Whyncha just get outta here? And write me that copy, fast."

I got out of there. Looking at him was reminding me of my own troubles.

I left the Concord in the parkade, dreaming of its bygone youth, and walked back through Pacific Centre, cut through Eaton's and came out on Robson Street at Howe. Two blocks over, past the art gallery and Duthie's bookstore, was Burrard Street and the downtown branch of the Vancouver Public Library.

The VPL is a freelancer's best friend. You can walk in

off the street, go up to a desk and instantly put to work a trained professional researcher, the kind of skilled fact hunter you'd have to pay fifty or sixty dollars an hour on the open market.

I'd done it a lot in the past and I did it again now. Ten minutes after I hit the business and government section on the second floor, a young woman with that air of calm control that librarians wear so well handed me a stack of books, journal pieces and newspaper clippings. I sat down at a table to become an instant expert on platinum.

More precisely, I learned more than I had already picked up from the occasional writing jobs I'd done for gold and silver mining companies and the lead-zinc giant, Cominco. I found out that there were a number of metals in the platinum group. Some of them I'd heard of, like chromium, and some of them sounded like planetary names from *Star Trek*, like vanadium.

They were used for more than just making jewellery: for example, you couldn't build a jet engine without platinum group alloys. But although they had crucial strategic value to commerce and defence, almost all the platinum ore deposits in Canada and the United States were too low grade to be mined. So more than a billion dollars was spent every year to import the stuff from southern Africa, the only place outside the Soviet Union where platinum could be found in rich lodes.

Clearly anybody who came up with a way to extract platinum group metals from low-yield North American deposits at a reasonable cost would make millions, probably hundreds of millions. If the Weasel's scientists were telling the truth, a piece of their process was worth far more than a share in any gold mine.

I looked at the names and address on the paper Geisel had given me. Rafe Byfield and Mike Polowicz were working out of an industrial park out on the Lougheed Highway in suburban Burnaby. It was time to find out whether the Weasel was fronting for a couple of genuine King Midases or just another pair of dream spinners ready to ply their shears on the VSE's perennial crop of lambs.

Three

THE INDUSTRIAL PARK was a square kilometre of small-to medium-sized buildings, flat-topped and utilitarian in design, each with grey cinder-block walls and a loading dock closed by a folding steel door painted royal blue. Some of the leased premises sported eye-catching signs that bespoke their owners' business ambitions; some had discreet plaques on or beside their doors.

Number 22 had nothing but the bare numerals stencilled in black on the smaller metal door next to the loading dock. I parked in the empty bay, climbed the concrete stairs and tried the lock.

It didn't budge. I rapped my knuckles on the metal. It was thick; I doubted the sound of my knocking carried far, so when no immediate answer came, I hammered with my fist.

I waited and was about to try a few kicks when the lock clicked. The door opened a hand's breadth, and a narrow, suspicious face looked me up and down. He was in his mid-thirties, blond with nondescript features except for eyes like chunks of green glass that said I wouldn't enjoy being tied up in this guy's basement.

"Yes? What do you want?" The accent was unusual; I couldn't place it.

I told him my name. "I'm the writer Len Geisel hired to do your brochure for the investors."

He didn't blink, and his eyes stayed tight on my face. He might have been memorizing the pattern of pores in my nose.

I showed him Geisel's piece of paper. "This is High Country Mining, isn't it? Are you Rafe Byfield or Mike Polowicz?"

He took the paper from my hand. At the top was printed "From the desk of Leonard Geisel," with the Weasel's scrawl underneath. He looked at it, turned it over, didn't give it back.

"Wait," he said and closed the door. I heard the lock click.

John Milton once observed that "they also serve who only stand and wait." I now served in that fashion for a good five minutes, feeling increasingly ridiculous, until the door cracked open a few centimetres again.

This time, the man who looked me over had a patriotic face: sun-reddened skin, prematurely white hair and pale blue eyes. He was older than his partner, pushing sixty, and had the kind of smooth assurance I had encountered in senior civil servants and other long-service professionals.

I said my name and handed him my card.

He took it and carefully read each word on it, then looked at me again. "You are a writer."

"Yes," I said. My speechwriter's ear picked up the same odd accent, vaguely mid-Atlantic, but with the vowels flattened — maybe New Zealand, I thought.

"What do you write?"

"Speeches, annual reports, brochures. Len Geisel hired me to do a brochure for your company. For when it gets listed on the stock exchange."

He digested that as if he were cross-examining a witness in court. "Len Geisel hired you," he said. "And where and when did this happen?"

"At his office in the Stock Exchange Tower, couple hours ago. He said he would phone, tell you I was coming. Look, is there a problem here?"

"I don't know. Is there?"

"You are either Mr. Byfield or Mr. Polowicz, right? You do know what I'm talking about?"

He said nothing.

"Tell you what, how about I come in and phone Len Geisel? I mean, if you're worried about industrial espionage or something, he can vouch for me."

His lips shaped a very small smile. "Why would I be worried about industrial espionage, Mr. Rafferty?"

"Well, because of the process, I guess. I saw the cube of platinum you made ... "

"Mr. Geisel showed it to you?" he interrupted.

"Yes. Look, let me come in and call him, and we can..."

"I can't let you come in, Mr. Rafferty."

I was starting to feel a little foolish. "OK," I said. "How about if I go find a phone somewhere else and have Mr. Geisel call you? He can give you a full description of me, I'll come back, and then maybe we can talk. How's that?"

He thought about it. "That would be fine."

"OK, I'll be right back." I turned and started down the stairs.

"There's no need to hurry, Mr. Rafferty," he said to my back. I heard the lock click again.

Two kilometres or so back down the Lougheed toward Vancouver was a Shell station with a pay phone. I dialled Geisel's cellular number and he answered as if his finger had been hovering over the talk button.

When he heard my voice he sounded disappointed. "Look," he said, "I'm waiting for a really important call here. I can't tie up the phone."

"You look," I said. "I didn't come all the way over from Comox to check out the pay phones in darkest Burnaby. Your High Country guys wouldn't tell me if my hat was on fire. Now you got to call them and tell them I'm not a goddamn bad guy and they can talk to me."

"Give me five," he said. "I'll call 'em, straighten 'em out."

I went into the gas station and bought myself an Eatmore bar. Then I sat in the Concord and listened to an oldies station. Louis Armstrong was singing about what a wonderful world it was back in the sixties.

Funny thing, but nobody I knew remembered that song from the sixties. Everybody had heard it for the first time in a 1980s movie in which the characters got nostalgic about their sixties experiences.

Then I guess some Generation X programming ace from Dallas or L.A., some kid who was still doing Pablum when the Beatles broke up, caught the movie and decreed that Satchmo had to make the list of middle-of-the-bell-curve AM hits that now defined for all time the weirdest decade of the twentieth century.

Nobody was asking me, but I figured that any retrospective of sixties music that included Louis Armstrong but left out the Fugs was as authentic as Brian Mulroney's humility.

Roger Gambowsky had told me once that I seemed to have strong opinions on just about everything.

"So?" I said. "What's wrong with having strong opinions?"

"It's just that they always seem to be strongly negative."

I'd shrugged off Roger's insight with some quick quip but I wondered later if he was right. Maybe I was turning into a sour old man before I even hit my forties. If so, it was because my thirties hadn't exactly been a day at the beach.

I finished the Eatmore and retraced my route to the industrial park. High Country Mining looked no more inviting than it had the first time, but I hoped the Weasel had clued in Byfield and Polowicz that I wasn't Emil Goldfinger or whatever dire threat they suspected I might be.

I nosed the car into the loading bay, killed the engine, undid my seat belt and got out. I was holding the driver's side handle, about to slam it closed, when the big blue folding door suddenly left the side of the building and rushed at me, haloed in black smoke. It slammed down onto the Concord's hood and roof like a slap from a steel giant. The impact drove the wagon back half a metre or more and spun me off my feet, sending a stab of agony down my left arm.

I dropped to my knees. The pain in my arm was astonishing. Horizontal bars of light flashed across my vision. Then there was pressure in my ears, as if someone had shoved his thumbs into them right down to the eardrums and leaned in with all his weight.

Some great beast was roaring beside me, and the light began to fade. I'm blacking out, I thought, and then I realized that my eyesight was fine. The light was dimming because the sky was blocked by a pall of thick oily smoke, shot through with dull red flames.

The Concord's door was open. It seemed sensible to crawl back in. My injured left arm wouldn't move properly, so I left the door flapping and forgot about the seat belt — I didn't plan to go far. I couldn't see ahead because the pleated metal door was draped over the front of the car. That was OK too: I wasn't planning on going forward.

I keyed the ignition, put the wagon into reverse, floored the pedal and spun the wheel. The Concord shot backwards in a curve, the steel door sliding from the hood. The hole in the building where the door had been was belching thick gobbets of smoke and tongues of flame. I backed the car farther off and stumbled out.

Although I was now twenty metres from the burning building, the beast was still roaring in my ears. Then it began to make a high-pitched whine like the last sustained note in Eric Clapton's solo on "Layla."

I looked around to see where the sound was coming from and saw a guy in coveralls opening and closing his mouth; it took me a few seconds to realize that he was shouting at me and that I was deaf.

I shook my head and tapped my ear. He gave up and turned toward the building. I supposed he'd been asking me if any people were in there. If they were, they wouldn't be coming out for a while. Not until the ashes were soaked right through.

The guitar note now gave way to a rushing sound like wind in the stand of second-growth firs behind my house overlooking the Puntledge Delta. I turned to see where the noise was coming from, but it was suddenly very dark and I was unaccountably sitting down and slowly, slowly falling backwards.

Some sadist was pounding a drum right behind me, and with each thudding beat an accomplice tore at my left shoulder with glowing hot pincers. I opened my eyes and saw a young woman looking down at me in professional appraisal. A stethoscope hung around her neck.

"Hi," I said.

"Headache?" she asked.

"No."

"How many fingers?"

"Two."

She took my head in her hands and rotated it, watching my eyes. "Did you hit your head?"

"No. My arm hurts."

"Good," she said. "Looks like no concussion. Your shoulder's dislocated. I'll just give you this, and then we'll put you back together again."

I felt a pinprick in my arm muscle, then a coolness stole up my neck and into my cranium like calamine on a bad sunburn. The drummer and his partner went off into a dark corner where I could hardly hear them. I inhaled a long, luxurious breath and let it go.

"What was that?" I asked the doctor.

"Demerol," she said.

"Can you get more of it?"

"Yes."

"Wonderful. Will you marry me?"

She smiled. "A policeman wants to talk to you," she said. "Do you feel up to it?"

"Sure," I said. "Ask him if he's got any Demerol."

They must be getting cops from a new supplier these days. They were clearly phasing out the traditional middle-aged slab of pork with rolls of bristle-covered flesh on the back of the neck. Now the force was stocked with sinewy young yuppie clones who looked like racquetball fanatics.

The Burnaby RCMP constable who peered down at me could have been taking a break between sets. "Mr. Rafferty," he said. "Can you tell me what happened?"

I told him. As the Demerol really kicked in, I was occasionally distracted by a small green thing with wings that kept appearing on the Mountie's shoulder. But I found that I could ignore it if I kept staring at the space between the cop's eyebrows. I told him about Geisel and the brochure and the two guys who didn't want to talk to me about platinum. I told him about the blue door coming to see me. I don't think I mentioned Louis Armstrong.

After a while the green thing on his shoulder started talking to me and I realized that I had lost track of what I was saying. Then I noticed that I was floating over a landscape of geometric mandalas outlined in red and black and shot through with brilliant flashes of electric blue light. There was something big on the horizon, all cream and gold, and I flew toward it.

The detective waiting for me when I got back was one of the older-model cops: a big, rough ovoid with a face that could have been carved from a potato, topped by an ear-to-ear, pretend-I'm-not-bald comb-over.

"Conroy," he said. "Coordinated Law Enforcement Unit."

I knew about CLEU. Way back in my political days, I'd been staff speechwriter to the federal minister of justice when the special investigations unit was set up. It was a clearing house for combined action by provincial Crown prosecutors, federal Mounties and local police forces; it built files on organized crime.

I was in a private room with a view looking south toward the evergreens in Burnaby's Central Park, now shaded almost black against a twilight sky. I tried to sit up in bed, but not all of me was connected to my head. The walls moved in mysterious ways. I sank back.

"Here," Conroy said and stooped to crank the handle at the foot of the bed. I rose like a drawbridge to a forty-five-degree angle. He brought over a chair and sat down, took out a notebook and looked at me. He had perfected the Joe Friday deadpan stare.

"Are you ready to talk to me?"

"Dry mouth," I croaked. "Need a drink."

A plastic carafe and tumbler sat on the table beside the bed. He reached, poured and handed me the water. I swallowed the lukewarm liquid, taking my time because all the while I was fast-forwarding through my involvement in Geisel's affairs, trying to decide if I might in any way have stepped over the line into the territory of accessory.

"You've had enough," said the cop. "Let's talk." He looked at his notes. "You are a writer. You were hired by Leonard Geisel to write about High Country Mining. You went to see Rafe Byfield and Mike Polowicz this afternoon. As you drove in there was an explosion and you sustained minor injuries."

"I don't know about the minor, but the rest sounds right," I said.

"Oh, does it?"

"What do you mean?"

His face told me he had definite views about who would ask the questions and who would answer them. "Did you talk to Byfield or Polowicz before the explosion?"

"Not really." I took another sip of the water. "They wouldn't let me in."

He made a note, then gave me the Joe Friday fish-eye. "They wouldn't let you in. But I thought the explosion occurred as you were parking your car."

I explained about making two trips. He took more notes.

"Did you see anybody else at the building on your first visit?"

"No."

"Were there any cars parked outside?"

I tried to remember and then said I didn't think so.

"Did Byfield and Polowicz seem nervous?"

"Very," I said.

"Do you know any reason why they might have been nervous?"

I told him what I knew about the platinum-extraction process and how it would be worth a lot of money. "Perhaps they were worried about someone stealing the formula or whatever it is." I didn't mention that anybody who put his future in the hands of the Weasel had every right to be nervous. "You should ask Len Geisel. He knew them; I didn't."

Conroy got up. "We'd like to ask Mr. Geisel about a number of things. Do you happen to know where he is?"

I said he'd either be at his office in the Stock Exchange
Tower, at his condo on False Creek or in a bar on Howe
Street.

Conroy watched to see how I reacted as he said, "He
didn't go home today, and his secretary hasn't seen him since
she went for lunch. He's got a cellular phone but he doesn't
answer." He closed his notebook. "He a friend of yours?"

"Just a client."

"Uh-huh. Well, if you see him, tell him we'd like to talk
to him." He turned to leave, then turned back. "Soon."

I finished the water and wondered what kind of mess
the Weasel had folded himself into. And whether I was still
just a spectator.

By 8:30 the next morning I was getting on the bus outside the hospital, my shoulder and arm judged too healthy
to be in a hospital bed when it was needed by somebody
who was really sick. The intern who checked me out after
breakfast said the only reason they'd put me in a private
room was because Conroy had told them to.

I dropped a loonie and a quarter in the fare box, got a
transfer and sat down with the morning paper I'd picked
up in the hospital lobby. I was on page five, being loaded
into an ambulance. There were no pictures of Byfield or
Polowicz; I gathered from the text that they were now

mostly charcoal, and the authorities would have to wait for dental records before the remains could be properly identified. The cause of the blast was unknown, but the Burnaby RCMP were speculating that volatile chemicals stored in the building might have been ignited by a Bunsen burner.

Byfield and Polowicz were described as American mining experts. I was down as a representative of the firm of Geisel, Chelmsford. I wondered if that reference gave me grounds for a libel suit.

The police impound yard was near the cop shop by Deer Lake. A new-model cop had me fill in and sign some forms, handed me my keys, then showed me where the Concord squatted nursing its wounds. The flying steel door had dented the hood just over the grill and gouged some paint off the roof. I thought it gave the car character, but that's also what I thought about the missing hubcaps and the two-by-four that propped up the back of the driver's seat.

I headed back to Geisel's office to see if I could find him and clarify the status of the High Country Mining brochure, but all I found was his secretary of the month, reading a paperback. The cover showed a ponytailed body builder with a truly huge nose invading the personal space of a sulky, tumble-haired young woman in off-the-shoulder lace. The secretary levered her eyes away long enough to say that her boss hadn't come in and hadn't called in. She indicated the pile of pink telephone message slips building on her desk.

I borrowed a phone and dialled Geisel's cellular number. A computer told me that the customer was apparently out of reach or just not answering. While I was still on Geisel's nickel, I called home to my answering machine, then tapped in the four-digit code that cajoled it into playing its cassette tape. There were two calls from the bank, one early yesterday and one late in the afternoon, as well as a gentle inquiry from the phone company about the overdue bill.

And then there was Karen's voice at the end of the tape. "Might have a job for you, if you're interested. Political work, of course. Call me at the office."

It made me think. I thought about the two calls from the banker, the impending flank attack by the phone company and the near certainty that the other thousand bucks I'd hoped to get out of Geisel had gone up in the same smoke that had consumed Byfield and Polowicz. Then I dialled the number she'd left on my machine and asked to speak to my ex-wife.

Most people's first impression of my ex-wife is that she's small, pretty and has more bounce than a Romanian gymnast. My first impression was that I was sure I already knew her but couldn't quite remember where or when we'd met.

The odd thing was that she had the same initial take on me. It wasn't until we'd spent several minutes comparing biographies and lists of friends that we realized we were perfect strangers who somehow felt as if we'd known each other all our lives.

My second impression was that I couldn't live without her. But two years and two children later, she would tell me I'd just have to try.

We met on a Monday morning in the Parliament Hill office of the Liberal minister of justice. We had both come bright and early for our first day in new jobs: I was the new speechwriter, a politically uncommitted hired gun from the press gallery; she was the new private secretary, an Ottawa veteran of two years and a card-carrying Liberal since her poli-sci days at UBC.

We liked the same music, books and movies. We had the knack of finishing each other's sentences. If they'd given out Nobel Prizes for sexual chemistry, we'd have been high on the short list. We didn't know that was all we had, a strange and temporary hankering for each other that would wear thin and leave nothing underneath. Our hunger for each other hid the reality that we were of different species: she was the daughter of a senior corporate lawyer, raised in a big house, educated in private schools, sent to Europe for a year before university; I was a labourer's son, raised in rented squalor, self-educated in public libraries where I used to go to get free of the hum of constant bickering that filled my parents' house between flare-ups into shrieking, cursing, tear-spraying fights.

None of that registered on Karen and me. We entranced each other. We married and within a year we had the twins; we named them William for her father and Richard for mine, although we always called them Bill and Dick. Then Karen spent a tiring ten months at home, breastfeeding and diaper changing, while I worked the crazy hours that are routine for ministers' staff.

By the time I was into my third year in Ottawa, she'd had enough of full-time motherhood. And I'd had enough of blizzards and freezing rain alternating with heat waves and humidity so dense the sky turned green. Besides, it was the spring of 1979, and everybody knew the Trudeau government was going down.

"I've got a job offer in Vancouver," I told her, standing in the hall of our rented brick duplex. Melted sleet pooled on the doormat as I set my suitcase down; I'd just come back from a ministerial trip to the west coast. "Guy I used to know when I worked on the *Sun* is heading up the PR department at WestCan Forest Products. Needs a writer. The job's mine for the asking."

Karen turned and went down the hall to the kitchen, where the kids were teething on brightly coloured plastic shapes in their mesh playpen. She stood looking down at

them, her back to me. "I don't want to leave Ottawa," she
said. "I'm thinking about getting back to work."

I took off my dripping coat and draped it over a chair.
"Where? The government's finished. As soon as they drop
the election writ you can start counting down two months
until we're all out on our butts."

She didn't turn, didn't say anything. I came over, put my
arms around her from behind. Her waist was slender again,
her stomach almost as hard and flat as when she'd been a
teenager riding in gymkhanas.

"Look," I said. "I know you're going nuts stuck at home
with the little guys. How about you work on the campaign
for a local candidate? Who knows, maybe Keith Davey pulls
off a miracle, Trudeau gets back in, and we decide what to
do then."

She still didn't say anything, didn't say that it was more
than just wanting to get back to work. Our chemistry set
was busted, but neither one of us could deal with it.

Senator Keith Davey had been the Liberals' best strategist in the 1970s, scoring electoral coups that won him
the nickname The Rainmaker. But the old fox couldn't
make it rain for the Liberals in the spring of 1979. When
the votes were counted, Joe Clark went to 24 Sussex Drive,
and Karen and I went back to Vancouver. She flew with
the twins; I drove a U-Haul rent-a-truck tightly packed with
everything we owned.

Behind the truck, bouncing along on a bumper tow-bar, was an almost new AMC Concord, the station wagon model, done in fake wood and cheerful yellow paint. I figured it would be perfect for holding two kids in car seats, with plenty of room in the back for diaper bags and fold-up strollers. I'd got the car cheap from a Canadian Press photographer I'd known casually for a couple of years. While going through a nasty divorce, he was selling off just about everything he owned at bargain-basement prices and immediately converting the proceeds into booze-ups for friends at the press club. He called it liquidation of assets and he seemed to gain new friends every night.

I took the job with WestCan and started learning about the forest industry. Karen signed on as a political consultant to a PR firm with Liberal connections. Her boss was Lyle Pastorel, who had become a name to conjure with in Grit Ottawa. He had been Mr. PMO — Prime Minister's Office, that is — to British Columbia Liberals since playing a big part in getting seven of them elected to Parliament in the anti-NDP backlash of 1974.

I didn't like Pastorel. He was slick as heavy crude on a shingle beach. Thousand-dollar suits and red suspenders, and if he ever lowered his braying voice long enough to let the room get quiet, you'd hear the ticking of his tin reptile's heart.

Karen thought he was a brilliant political strategist and said so. She also thought, but didn't say, that he was the man she should have married. She was right both times.

Joe Clark managed to hold it together for the Tories for only nine months. Then he unaccountably failed to feed the handful of Quebec Creditiste MPs their customary sop.

The Creditistes were the rump of a once moderately influential federal political party that had formerly held several seats in Quebec and the west. Now they were reduced to a scattering of ridings in Quebec dairy country. The MPs' sole *raison d'être* was to squeeze out of Ottawa an extra half-cent or so per litre on the subsidy to the dairy farmers who reliably elected them.

When Joe Clark failed to deliver the customary Danegeld, the five Creditiste MPs withheld their support in the crucial vote on John Crosby's budget, and Joe was suddenly just a footnote to history.

The Liberals were ready with an instant comeback effort. Karen worked tirelessly on the B.C. portion of the campaign. She was always at Pastorel's elbow, his keeper of the poll results, his soother of nervous candidates. She was good at it, a natural who was finally getting a chance to show what she could do. I spent a few evenings stuffing envelopes and writing candidate bios for the central campaign, but most of my time now was for work and the kids.

Election day came and the Liberals stomped the Tories east of the Manitoba border. By the time the polls closed on the west coast, Trudeau was mounting a stage at the Chateau Laurier, flashing that vulpine grin and saying, "Welcome to the 1980s." I put the kids to bed and waited up for Karen, finally falling asleep in the living room while the CBC's political correspondents went around and shot the wounded.

She woke me at 3:30 a.m., flushed, happy, eyes sparkling the way I used to see them early in the morning after we'd made love all night.

"Isn't it great?" she said.

"Yeah," I said. And it was great to see her so totally alive, all systems optimum. She was a thoroughbred that had just won the derby and knew it.

She took a deep breath, held it for a beat, then used it all quickly, saying, "He offered me a job."

I blinked and sat up. The room was cold. "Pastorel?" I asked.

She paced the floor, her palms slapping a rapid little drumbeat on her thighs. "A policy desk at PMO. Real work, Sid. We're going to give this country a constitution."

It's funny how you can ignore an impending unpleasant reality right up until it bumps its belly into your nose. What did I think was going to happen if the Liberals got back into power? Apparently nothing; I'd gone through the campaign not letting myself see the inevitable outcome, but now here it was, banging on my forehead and telling me to listen up.

"I guess we'd better talk," I said.

"I told him yes," said Karen.

"You told him yes." So much for talking.

"I want the job, Sid. It's what I want to do. It's what I'm going to do."

"I don't want to go back to Ottawa."

"I know."

A silence grew between us until finally I said, "So ... what happens now?"

She didn't say anything, just walked out of the room. A few days later, she walked out of my life and caught the red-eye to Ottawa, leaving me with a leased condo on the soon-to-be-fashionable Fairview Slopes, the twins and her monthly support cheque that paid the nanny who'd been looking after Bill and Dick more than either of us the past couple of months.

We pretended, incredibly enough, that nothing serious was happening. We made lighthearted remarks about long-distance marriage, talked glibly about our being strengthened by a little time away from each other. It was all an empty bubble of words, but we had gotten wonderfully good at batting it back and forth without ever hitting it so hard it would go pop.

So off she went to Ottawa, and we talked on the government WATS line every day at first, and then every other
day, and then it was once in a while, till one day the phone
rang and it was Karen, and she was sorry, but she wanted a
divorce so she could marry Pastorel.

And she wanted the kids.

"No," I said. "That asshole is not going to raise my sons."

But he did. The next voice I heard was her lawyer's, and
he was of the kind who inspire all those jokes, you know
the ones, like "What's the difference between a lawyer and
a great white shark? The shark will often be satisfied with
just ripping off your leg."

I was willing to fight the lawyer, but midway through
his careful escalation of threats and pressure, the worst
recession in fifty years whacked the forest industry flat.
WestCan's senior executives were of that breed of straight-
line-thinking engineers that used to run B.C. forest companies back when increasing production was the only
challenge. They showed the industry's usual knee-jerk reaction when faced with a sudden downturn: they fired the
public-relations department.

I had not been with the company long enough to merit
a severance parachute. I was out in the cold no-man's-land
of unemployment, and it was the era of Reaganomics. I
wasn't sure I could feed myself, never mind two toddlers. I
let Karen take them on two conditions: they would keep my

name and remain Raffertys, and I would have them for one month every summer.

That was in 1981. In the summer of 1984 Mulroney led the Tories back into the best offices on Parliament Hill. The Pastorels moved back to the coast. I was freelancing, without much commitment or much success. We'd run into each other at the PR society luncheons and be cordial. It was all very civilized.

And very civilized was just how Karen now looked, in perfectly suitable grey silk, as she wound her way toward me through Pastorel's open-concept office. It was on a pricey floor of a pricey commercial tower with metallic windows that reflected the traffic on West Georgia back at itself and tinted the view from within so that, looking out, you would think the streets really were paved with gold.

She pecked my cheek, smelling like a cloud out of heaven. I followed her to a corner office, where she waved me to a seat on a leather-covered couch and sat down in a nice little brocaded chair. The assistant brought us pure Kona in good china and left, closing the door.

"Are you all right?" she said, touching her forehead and gesturing to the bump and butterfly bandage on mine. "I saw the story when I got to the office and I called the hospital, but you had already checked out."

I said I was OK and asked after the boys. She told me how they were doing in their up-market private school that

I could never have afforded. I smiled and didn't wince. We did small talk for a couple of minutes, then she said, "I guess you could use some work."

"What makes you say that?"

"The hundred-dollar cheque you sent the boys for their birthday. It bounced."

This time I couldn't stop the wince in time.

"It's OK, Sid. I covered it."

I didn't know where to look. "There's a wrinkle in the movie deal," I said.

She looked at me with real affection. Sometimes I hated that most of all. "I asked around," she said. "Your deal fell through. You need work."

"I don't want to work for Pastorel," I said.

"He feels the same way about you," she said. "I insisted that we call you."

"He doesn't want me here?"

"If you want to be blunt about it."

"Good. What do you need me for?"

"To write some first-rate political material. And not get caught up in any partisan complications."

"You need a mercenary," I translated. "Somebody who stays bought."

"If you like." She looked at me over her coffee cup. I still liked the way her eyes laughed. "We'll need all the usual campaign stuff — letters to the editor for supporters to sign and send in, fact sheets, a candidate bio, an op-ed piece tailored for the up-country weeklies and maybe for one of the Vancouver dailies. And a couple of very good, very carefully crafted speeches."

"Interesting," I said, because it was. "Who's the candidate and what's he running for?"

She sipped her coffee and leaned back. "I won't tell you the candidate's name ... not yet. But he'll be running for premier."

I almost dropped my cup. "You mean Vander Zalm's stepping down?"

"No. We're staging a coup."

Four

——

PASTOREL OPENED KAREN'S door without knocking and stuck his costly coiffure into the room. "Room for one more?"

He was asking Karen, but I answered first. "Why not?"

He eased in and sat on a corner of her desk, wearing his Armani the way kings used to wear their regalia, flaunting his elevation above the ordinary ruck. He gave me a number two smile, but it was no big deal; he had plenty of them.

"Hey, what's happening in the movie biz?" he said.

I looked at Karen. She gave a tiny shake of her head. I hated feeling grateful that she hadn't told him.

"The movie biz is great," I lied. "I'm working up a new project."

"Oh yeah?"

"It's the world's first rap opera, based on the life of the Waltz King of nineteenth century Vienna. It's called *Yo, Strauss!*"

Karen gave me a knock-it-off look, then turned to gaze out the window.

Pastorel cocked his head to one side. "Sometimes I can't tell when you're kidding," he said.

"Sometimes neither can I."

"So, did Karen fill you in?"

"Just a tease. You want to topple the government."

He gave me a number one smile. "No, not the government. Just the guy sitting on top of it. The guy who's fucking it up for everybody."

Other Canadians want their politicians to be as bland as boiled eggs. British Columbians prefer a spicy dash of idiosyncrasy at the top.

The tradition started early. One of the province's first premiers began his career as just plain Bill Smith, a prospector in the California gold rush of '49. Fed up with general delivery postal clerks giving his mail away to the dozens of other Bill Smiths who flourished in the gold fields, he renamed himself Amor de Cosmos — literally, Lover of the Cosmos — before moving north to go into journalism, politics and ultimately a madhouse.

In 1989 the province had two living ex-premiers. Bill Bennett, the Kelowna tough guy whose budget-slashing "restraint program" had brought the province to the brink

of a general strike, was engaged in a lot of legal manoeu-
vring these days, trying to get out from under charges of
insider trading in shares of a major lumber company run by
an old family friend.

Dave Barrett, after a long career as a heart-on-his-sleeve
social democrat, had taken a stall in the stable of flamboyant radio talk-show hosts at CJOR, an AM station owned by
the self-made billionaire and arch-capitalist Jimmy Pattison.
Pattison was thought to have spent heavily to defeat Barrett's
short-lived NDP government, but radio made strange
bedfellows.

The present premier, Bill Vander Zalm, made even
his most colourful predecessors look like straight-arrow
Mormon accountants. When he was campaigning for the
Social Credit leadership, his opponents spoke darkly of a
loose cannon on the decks of government. Once he became
premier, Vander Zalm's cannon turned out to be worse than
loose. He eventually got his muzzle pointed down into the
bowels of his own ship and kept firing round after round
through the hull. The bewildered Socreds, a genially cyn-
ical alliance of Liberal and Conservative forces dedicated to
keeping the left-wing New Democratic Party out of power
in the province, were spending more and more time bailing
to keep themselves afloat.

It was now three years since Vander Zalm had finessed
the party out from under a clutch of Socred heavies at the

glitzy 1986 leadership convention held in the ski resort community of Whistler. The media had covered his bid to lead the party and the subsequent general election as if the Dutch-born populist with the movie-star looks were a combination of Michael Jackson and a particularly charismatic pope. It was a Socred landslide. But once the votes were counted, British Columbians found they had elected the most wacko political circus the province had ever seen.

Vander Zalm's disenchanted friends in the media — the same ones who had helped him glad-hand to election victory — now took to calling him Willy Wooden Shoes, as the energetic premier strove to outdo Mad King Ludwig of Bavaria as an architect of strange political initiatives. He privatized Crown agencies almost at random, named favourite cabinet ministers as regional czars but neglected to give them any actual authority, frequently announced economic development projects that subsequently evaporated and flew off to his native Holland to star in a musical fantasy movie about St. Nicholas.

But the breaking point came when he cheerfully took on the abortion issue. Every sensible political leader in the country tiptoed around it. It was a no-winner, as I remembered from my stint in federal politics, when my boss had been faced with the question of what to do about Dr. Morgentaler.

But Vander Zalm waded in right up to his nostrils,

saying he saw nothing wrong with basing public policy on his private religious views.

The parliamentary opposition in the provincial legislature practically lit candles for Vander Zalm, imploring the patron saints of social democracy to keep him in office until they could wage an electoral war against him. The New Democrats, a left-wing coalition of labour, environmentalists and social progressives that had held power in B.C. for only two and a half years in a half-century, saw public disenchantment with the loose-lipped premier as their best chance to bust up the old Socred coalition once and for all.

The downtown suits who had bankrolled the free-enterprise Socreds for almost forty years would have gladly staked the premier out in the parking lot of the Vancouver Club and backed a Mercedes over him. As far as the boardroom crowd was concerned, Vander Zalm guaranteed two terms in office for the social democrats: and that would mean higher corporate taxes, a tougher labour code, new environmental laws and no more hot-and-cold running cabinet ministers whenever corporate B.C. needed something doing.

On October 3, 1989, alarmed at their plummeting poll numbers, four Socred backbenchers had publicly walked out of caucus and called for a leadership review. The media made a fuss about them. The march away from

Vander Zalm was now ready to set off; all it needed was a leader.

The Socreds had prospective leaders in abundance — including those who had gagged on Vander Zalm's dust at the leadership convention — but none of them wanted to be the one to put the knife in. Each of the premier's heirs presumptive was waiting for one of the others to be splashed with first blood.

Not because they were squeamish. Not because they were troubled by the prospect of being disloyal. It was because whoever belled the Vander Zalm cat would be swiftly pulled down and torn to scraps by the raging Zalmoids — Christian fundamentalists and pro-lifers — who now infested the party.

To save Social Credit, one of the party's leading figures would have to sacrifice his or her political career. But so far nobody around the cabinet table was offering to die for the cause. As for the four dissidents, they were starting to look like Wile E. Coyote at that moment when the engine of his Acme rocket-sled stalls a few metres out in the bright blue air beyond the cliff's edge.

The downtown business crowd were twitchy. If none of the obvious contenders within Social Credit had the moxie to make a move, then somebody had to be brought in from the outside. And I thought I could guess who it would be.

"It's Miggs, isn't it?" I said. "You got Miggs."

Pastorel looked at Karen, who shrugged, then back at me. "Why do you say that?"

"Because it's obvious. Jimmy Pattison might open his wallet but he's not going to give up being a billionaire to run the province for you. Rick Hansen's been around the world in a wheelchair and now he's got better things to do. Who else is there?"

Pastorel's face told me I was right. "Karen said I'd been underestimating you," he said.

"It happens."

"Yeah." He looked at me, and I guessed he was mentally taking me out of the "schmuck" file and putting me into some other category. "So, OK, it's Miggs. Are you all right with that?"

"Why not?"

Nothing was wrong with Anthony John Migliorini except for his legs. They hadn't worked since the August afternoon when he'd rappelled down into Lynn Canyon in mountainous North Vancouver to rescue some teenage moron who probably couldn't read the "KEEP AWAY — THIS PLACE WILL KILL YOU STONE DEAD" signs all along the lip of the precipice.

The kid had wanted to dive into the swirlpools of Lynn Creek, a rushing mountain stream that had sculpted the underlying rock into a hidden maze of deeps and deathtraps.

It was a popular form of Russian roulette that claimed an adolescent life or two each summer with monotonous regularity. Miggs had been thirty-four years old, an airport firefighter and champion rock climber. He was also a member of the North Shore Search and Rescue Team: one of those priceless human beings who voluntarily risk life and limb to get between idiots and the natural consequences of their stupidity.

The teenager had chickened out and was cowering on a ledge ten metres above the pool. Miggs had climbed down with a rope and harness, got them on the boy and signalled for the team to pull him up. He was climbing back up his own rope, parallelling the teenager's ascent, when the kid panicked and began to struggle, almost slipping out of the harness.

Miggs swung over, trying to calm the boy down, and the kid began to kick out. The first kick caught Miggs in the hip and spun him around so that the second kick thudded squarely into his lower back. There was a snap and a tear, and the firefighter's legs became two dangling hunks of meat and bone that would never move again.

The media did a few tongue-clucking stories. Somebody put Miggs up for a Governor General's medal. And then he was forgotten. Until about nine months later, when Miggs parked his wheelchair beside a downtown office block and proceeded to climb it. Using equipment he had designed and built himself, the paraplegic scaled sixty metres of corporate concrete, then tacked a homemade banner to the side of the tower. "NEVER STOP TRYING" was the message. Then he continued to the roof of the building, right into the lenses and microphones of the waiting media.

And he turned out to be just what they were looking for. He had the self-deprecating humour of Will Rogers, the quiet determination of Terry Fox and — they noticed for the first time — the beamish good looks of a movie star.

"Why did you climb the building?" a TV reporter asked.

"To get you to listen to me," said Miggs.

"What did you want to say?"

He ignored the reporters and looked directly into the camera. "I wanted you to know that you can do it," he told anybody who was watching. "If I can climb a building, you can quit smoking or learn to read or get along without people who don't give you respect. Just don't stop trying. Never stop trying."

They ran it on the six o'clock news, and the phones lit up like a fireworks display. The next morning Miggs was on the early TV shows, then the morning radio talkfests, then the noon news. He said the same thing into every microphone: "don't stop trying." He was simple, direct and perfect, and people couldn't get enough of him.

Then he stopped giving interviews, wouldn't answer his phone, dropped out of sight as quickly as he'd popped into public view. It was a week before a persistent reporter cornered him as he pushed his specially designed shopping cart around a supermarket.

"Why did you drop out of sight, Miggs?"

"I didn't have anything else to say."

"But you're a celebrity now."

"So what?" he said and wheeled away.

Nine months later he was suddenly back again. The adoptive mother of a sick little boy who needed a bone marrow transplant had written Miggs a letter asking him to talk to the kid, help him to hold on until they found a compatible donor.

Miggs did better than talk to the kid. He went out and climbed another building — an even bigger one. When the news crews showed up, he told them that he was checking into a clinic the next day to be tissue-typed as a bone marrow donor. And anybody who had a heart ought to do the same.

It all happened again: saturation radio, print and TV coverage as Miggs showed up at the clinic, went through a brief procedure and faced a media scrum in the parking lot.

A fierce blonde shoved her mike in his face. "Why did you decide to help the little boy?"

Miggs's expression said it was a stupid question but his tone was pure patience. "Wouldn't you help a sick kid if you could?"

"Well, sure."

"Good. Then stop talking to me, get in there and get tested."

She did. So did a few thousand other people over the next few days. One of them was an exact match for the sick kid; he got his transplant and got better. Miggs dropped out of sight again.

That had been the pattern for almost three years. Every now and then Miggs would pull some stunt to gain attention, make whatever point he felt needed to be made, charm and disarm the media for forty-eight hours, then slip back into obscurity. He was a one-man commando raid on public opinion but somehow he never wore out his cachet. In the tracking polls he always scored among the top two or three people most admired by the man in the street.

Most politicians would roll in broken glass if it would get them Miggs's popularity numbers, and all parties had quietly approached him about running for a seat. He had turned them down, saying he was too busy adjusting to his new way of life.

And now Pastorel had him. It was like Niccolo Machiavelli managing St. Francis of Assisi.

"Has he given you a commitment?" I wanted to know.

Pastorel gave me his blandest look. "He has indicated a willingness to serve if conditions are right."

"What conditions?"

"You don't need to know that right now."

He was right; I was just being nosy. He said he would leave it to Karen to brief me on what I did need to know and went off to do something more important than talk to me.

Karen didn't have much to brief me with. She gave me a wad of newspaper clippings and a biographical summary of Miggs that one of Pastorel's researchers had put together.

"Start your clock, you're on the payroll," she said. "Read the background. Before things start to move, I'd like to send you up the coast to Sechelt" — I knew that that was where Miggs was running some kind of rehab camp — "put the two of you together, maybe for a couple of days, so you can really get to know each other."

"I'd like that," I said. I finished my coffee and put the china cup on her desk. "But something is not adding up here."

"What do you mean?"

"Well, I appreciate the work and all, ma'am, but I don't see Migliorini really mixing with a ghostwriter. Or going to work for a bunch of political hustlers like" — I was going to say Pastorel but I caught it — "like us."

She shrugged again, got up and looked down at the afternoon traffic. "He'll have his reasons. *My* reason is that I want him to have the best backup we can provide."

I doffed an imaginary hat. "Thank you kindly."

She turned back to me. "Also, at some point he may need someone around him who's not just a hustler. If he's only trying to do some good, I don't want him to get hurt."

"OK." I got up, tucked the bumf under my arm and reached for the door.

"And, Sid, one more thing."

"What?"

"Some of the Zalmoids are ... well, they're feeling threatened and they don't like it. They already know that this firm is working behind the scenes. Once we go public, anybody involved might be a target. So it wouldn't be good to have too high a profile."

I laughed. "What are they gonna do, picket my house?"

A little vertical line appeared above the bridge of her nose. "You're out of touch with the way the party's changed since Vander Zalm took over. Some of his real diehard supporters don't think it's going too far to toss firebombs at abortion clinics. To them this is not politics; it's holy war. When we start to push, they might get a little crazy. So watch out, Sid."

I'd left the car underneath Pacific Centre, so I walked the few blocks back from Karen's office. The light was red at Georgia and Howe. As I stood there with a gaggle of downtown pedestrians, all facing resolutely forward waiting for the green so they could get on with racing their particular rats, I heard a faint *click* beside me.

I turned to see a lightweight nondescript man in a lightweight nondescript suit tucking something small and dark into his pocket and turning to walk away.

"Hey!" I said. "Did you just take my picture?" He kept going, cutting across lawn toward the plaza surrounding the old courthouse that was now the Vancouver Art Gallery. I began to follow. "Hey! Hold on, I want to talk to you!"

He sped up, dodging between the panhandlers and street kids who hang around the kitschy seacoast-and-surf fountain that Ottawa laid on the city to celebrate the 1967 centennial of Confederation. I tried to follow, but a girl with a bedroll tied over her black leather jacket got in the way and said, "Spare change?"

By the time I stepped around her, the man was gone. I shrugged, which made my shoulder ache, and said the hell with it. It was probably one of Conroy's CLEU snoops padding out the file. If he needed my picture, he was welcome to it.

I ate a late lunch at the little bistro on Eaton's second floor and browsed through the Miggs file. It told me nothing I hadn't known but it reminded me of a few things I'd forgotten.

By now it was closing on two o'clock, my head was

throbbing and I just wanted to go home. But first I had to give Geisel's tree one more hopeful shake.

I went downstairs, through the mall and back up into the Stock Exchange Tower. Geisel's secretary was deeper into her bodice-ripper, the stack of message slips was thicker but the Weasel's office was just as empty. I tried his cellular number one more time but got the same nobody-home spiel from BC Tel's computer. There were no new nudges from the banker on my answering machine.

Afternoon traffic was building toward rush hour as I chugged through Stanley Park and over the bridge to West Vancouver and the ferry terminal. But I wouldn't be seeing the terminal for another hour or more.

It was a sunny Friday, so the tail end of the lineup for the two-hourly sailings was already a few kilometres from the ferry slip. My chances of catching the three o'clock sailing were nil, and it was iffy whether I'd be on the five o'clock boat.

I got in line, cut the engine, turned on the radio and put up with David Clayton Thomas singing "Hi-de-ho" for the umpteenth time. All the really good Blood Sweat and Tears cuts were on their first album, but the radio only played the pap the group had recorded after they'd become popular enough to cash in.

I punched the button and got CBC.Vicki Gabereau was interviewing somebody famous I'd never heard of, and I'd tuned in too late in the conversation to be sure what the guest was famous for. After five minutes of their enthusiastic sharing of views on nouvelle cuisine and the shiny, pointy roofs on new buildings, I was beginning to suspect the interviewee was of the modern breed of celebrity — that meant he could be celebrated just for being well known, without ever having done anything remarkable at all.

The radio voices blurred and faded, then a horn blast from behind shook me awake. The car ahead of me had moved on toward the terminal, and the guy behind wanted to follow. My watch said four-thirty. The lineup snaked slowly toward the ferry slip, and I was next to last onto the five o'clock sailing. The ramp went up and the giant boat rattled away from the dock. I slid over to the front passenger seat of the Concord — the one without a two-by-four propping it up — tilted it back and slept until the boat docked in Nanaimo just before seven.

Ninety minutes later, the twilight deepening the colour of the mountains, I eased up Ryan onto Back Road and pulled into my driveway. The car subsided with only a few mutters and one brief shake.

I just sat there for a half a minute, holding the steering wheel, too whacked to move. I'd driven the last twenty klicks straining to keep my eyes open and the Concord's headlights in the right lane. Finally I yawned, shook myself, got out and walked to the front steps.

I didn't remember leaving the front door open. Because I hadn't. The culprits were the Mongol mini-horde it must have taken to create so much chaos in so confined a space.

The place had been trashed. No, not trashed, I thought, as I began to pick details out of the jumble of furniture, stereo components, tapes and books — hundreds of books, strewn around the living room. Nothing that I could see was broken, but everything must have been picked up, turned over, opened, examined and searched.

I walked through into the kitchen. The mess was worse. Even the tea had been poured from its canister onto the counter, and the shelf paper left by the former owner was lying on the vinyl floor.

The rest of the house was like Arlo Guthrie's line from "Alice's Restaurant," "There wasn't no single part left untouched." When I got to the bedroom, I just swept the former contents of my closet onto the floor from where they had been thrown on the bed, lay face down and crashed. I'd call the cops in the morning.

In the dream I was in the dark. There were odd noises, muffled and ominous, but I couldn't make them out. They puzzled me at first, then suddenly I was frightened. A man said something indistinct next to me, and I turned to run. Then someone grabbed my arms and pinned them behind my back.

I woke up to find that someone had grabbed my arms and pinned them behind my back, while a big meaty hand pushed my face into the bed covers. I couldn't breathe. I kicked out but hit only air. Someone was binding my wrists with tape or cloth. I pulled against it, but the only result was a stab of pain through my torn shoulder ligaments.

The hand kept pushing me down. I sensed black unconsciousness welling up, panicked and arched my back, kicked again, then sucked in a long, marvellous breath as the pressure left the back of my head.

I was seized by my tethered wrists and pulled upright. The muscles in my shoulder were on fire. The bedroom was dim with predawn light, so dim I could see only that there were two of them, big guys who tossed me around like a medicine ball. I heard a ripping sound, then a band of sticky tape was slapped over my mouth, and I was pushed back down onto the bed. Another rip, and my ankles were lashed together.

Then I heard the slither of a long zipper being opened. Hands grabbed my knees and elbows and I was lifted, still face down, from the bed to an open sleeping bag they had spread on the floor.

When they zipped it up, my head was at the closed end and I was in the dark. I struggled a bit until a heavy hand slapped my head hard enough to make pain thunder behind my eyes.

"Don't make trouble," said a voice I recognized. It went with the Blue Stratos I'd inhaled when they'd first lifted me up. So I didn't make trouble, even when they carried me downstairs and put me in the trunk of the Cadillac.

Samuel Johnson used to say that when a man knows he is to be hanged in a fortnight, it concentrates his mind wonderfully. Being trussed up and carried off in a mobster's trunk had much the same effect on me. But, although I concentrated my best, I couldn't think of any reason why Lou Savelek was taking me for a ride. I just hoped he meant to bring me back. And in one piece.

My immediate concern was getting enough air to breathe way down in the bottom of Lou's sleeping bag. I stretched out in the Cadillac's roomy trunk, lifted my feet and parted my knees as much as possible, making a tunnel that let some air get through. It still smelled like Lou.

I could hear the whir of blacktop under the car's rear tires and I rolled one way or another whenever they took a corner. Then they slowed to make one careful turn, and the whir became a hiss punctuated by pocks as loose gravel ricocheted off the undercoat. The road got rougher, although the Caddie's suspension made riding in its trunk only slightly less smooth than sitting in the front seat of my Concord.

I felt the car slide around a curve and start to nose up a steep slope. I knew where we were going now. If they took the bag off me, I'd be getting my second look at Coronado.

The slope levelled off, we took one last corner and the Caddie stopped. I heard the doors open and shut with that satisfying big-car *thunk*, then the trunk opened and a little cool morning air seeped past my knees and into my nostrils. I could hear an engine whining, growing louder.

I was hauled out and stood upright, then the sleeping bag was unzipped and pulled away. I took a deep breath and a good look around. We were in the square of buildings I'd inspected on Tuesday. Savelek had a grip on my elbow to keep me from falling; the other guy was a shadowy blur behind the glass dome of a helicopter's cockpit. He apparently doubled as a pilot.

Lou took a buck knife from his pocket, opened it and gave me his dance-hall look again. Then he chuckled, stooped and cut the tape that bound my ankles. He pushed me toward the 'copter, and I struggled in with hands and arms still tied behind me. It was an eight-seater with benches facing fore and aft behind the pilot and copilot seats. Lou strapped me into the forward facing bench, cinching the seat belt tighter until I grunted to let him know he'd

hurt me. Then he sat on the other bench and reached over
his shoulder to tap the pilot on the back of the head. The
engine revved, the seat under me tilted forward and we
were airborne.

The 'copter rose swiftly away from Mount Washington
and arced gently toward the southeast, where the sun was
leaning on the far slopes of the Coastal Range before join-
ing us up here in the lonely sky. In a few minutes we over-
flew the hippie farms and artists' communes on Denman
and Hornby Islands and steered across the Strait of Georgia
toward the mainland.

I looked out the square window. We had levelled off at
what I guessed to be fifteen hundred metres. The sea below
us was grey and wrinkled like the skin of some giant, sluggish
beast that would swallow you without knowing or caring. I
looked at Lou, and he smiled. I preferred the view outside.

Vancouver International Airport has two passenger termi-
nals: the main facility, where the jumbos of national and
overseas carriers rub avionic shoulders with the twin-
engine jets and turboprops of regional lines; and the south
terminal, where small charter and private craft come and go.

The south terminal was where I'd used to come and go
myself, back when I was the justice minister's special assistant
for communications. I'd fly in on the comfy government

Lockheed JetStar so I could be there to hold the man's coat or distribute copies of his speaking text at a Law Society luncheon.

Often the government flight would be met by staff from the departmental office. But this early in the morning there weren't too many people around as the 'copter dropped down onto its circled H.

"Don't do nothing stupid," Savelek said. I nodded.

A grey windowless van crossed the tarmac and stopped beside us. A sliding door in the van's side opened, Savelek popped the 'copter door and frog-marched me the two metres between the aircraft and the vehicle. Thirty seconds after the 'copter landed, I was face down under a tarp in the back of the van, wondering where we were going. And who wanted to see me.

My nose told me where I was the moment Lou pulled back the tarp and opened the van door. The mingled smells of detergent suds, steam and bleach almost overpowered my captor's cologne. We were at the loading dock of a big laundry, one that probably handled linen for a slew of hotels and restaurants at prices the customers paid without arguing.

Lou grabbed my arm and moved me fast across the loading dock, past bales of sheets and towels wrapped in brown paper and sealed with tape. We went through a battered door, up a flight of concrete stairs and down a corridor with cinder-block walls painted institutional green. Then we came to a wooden door with a frosted glass panel bearing the word "PRIVATE" in faded paint.

He knocked, and a voice said, "Come in."

What was I expecting, Marlon Brando with cotton in his cheeks? Edward G. Robinson in spats? Whatever it was, it wasn't the neat and tidy little man in the simple suit behind the simple desk who looked up from a ledger book, first at me and then at Savelek. He put down an old-fashioned fountain pen and clasped his doll-like hands together on the desk.

"What is this shit?" he said, and I was glad that it was Lou and not me who was occupying the focal point of those dead, cold eyes. The man had not raised his voice above a conversational level.

Lou stiffened. Through my shirt sleeve I could feel his warm hand get suddenly moist. "What?" he said.

Now the voice had an edge, each syllable precisely enunciated, though the volume stayed down. "Get the fucking tape off the man's mouth! Cut him loose and get him a fucking chair!"

If I hadn't been so frightened, I would have enjoyed the sight of Savelek fairly scurrying to mollify the small man with the tiny hands clasped together like teacher's pet. But I figured if this guy scared Lou, then he ought to plain terrify me.

Lou cut me loose and brought a straight-backed oak

chair for me to sit on. He tried to gently strip the tape from my mouth, but it was just like in the movies. I pushed his hand away and ripped the tape free.

In the movies the hero winces when the tape comes off, the kind of wince that makes you think it's about as painful as a firm slap on a medium sunburn. In real life, the adhesive rips away the top layer of skin, and it feels just like a layer of skin is being torn from your living flesh.

Tears misted my vision, I ground my teeth and managed to count myself lucky that I had shaved off my moustache a few weeks earlier. I blinked, wiped away the tears with the back of my hand and looked up to find the little man watching me with his dark, empty eyes.

"Would you like some coffee?" he asked. My first impulse was to say no, but some part of my psyche must have been functioning at full paranoia, because all at once it occurred to me that this was not a man to say no to even under the most innocuous circumstances. And the present circumstances were anything but.

"Thank you, yes," I said. He told Savelek to bring coffee. Then he waited, saying nothing until Lou had come back in, deposited two styrofoam cups of strong black brew and then stood there like a stooge. There was nowhere for him to sit, and I was pretty sure he had never had the benefit of Milton's advice regarding the meritoriousness of standing and waiting.

The little man spoke to Lou slowly as if too many words per minute would clog up his intake system. "I told you, I want to see this Sid Rafferty. I didn't say nothing about you should cause him any trouble. Just bring him to me. Now I got to apologize to this man and I don't like it that you put me in this situation."

I sipped my coffee, keeping my eyes down.

"I'm sorry, Uncle Enzo," said Lou.

"Get outta here. Go help your cousin with the deliveries." Lou left, closing the door carefully behind him.

"I apologize for what has been done to you," the little man said. "My sister's boy. I try to give him something to do, but he gets too … " He moved his tiny hands as if waiting for the right word to drop into them.

"Enthusiastic?" I tried.

His index finger pointed at me, then folded with the others back on the top of the desk. "Exactly. You are a writer, you would know the right word. Enthusiastic."

I put the coffee on the desk and rubbed my shoulder, winced a little. The little man noticed. "He do that to you?"

"No. I was in an explosion."

He nodded. "I read that." He opened a drawer, took out a newspaper clipping and showed it to me. It was me being loaded into the ambulance. "This is you."

"Yes."

He took a pair of gold-rimmed reading glasses from the

drawer and put them on, holding the paper at arm's length. "It says 'representative of Geisel, Chelmsford.' That is what I want to talk to you about."

He took off the glasses and levelled his flat gaze on me again. His eyes were like unpolished stones; they didn't even seem to reflect light from the window. I said I would be happy to tell him anything he wanted to know.

"What is your connection to Geisel, Chelmsford?"

"I was hired by them to write a brochure about a mining company whose stock they were promoting. I was going to see the mining people when their building blew up."

He looked at me and said nothing for at least a minute. I managed to meet his eyes for about ten seconds, then I looked at his hands folded on the desk. They didn't move. Somewhere deep in the building, heavy machinery began to thrum. I swallowed another sip of coffee.

"How do you know Leonard Geisel?" he said.

"He's an occasional client."

"Is he a friend?"

"No."

He said nothing, just sat and looked at me while I fought an almost irresistible urge to squirm in my chair.

"I seen you somewhere, some other time."

"I don't think so."

"You don't think so. I *know* so." His face seemed to go completely blank now. I had the impression of a vast segmented store of memory behind those sterile eyes, row upon row of pigeonholes stuffed full of the myriad transactions of this man's life, with no debt uncollected, no trespass forgiven. His gaze came back into focus. He snapped his fingers and pointed at me again, and his head came down in a decisive nod. "Yeah, you come into the Wedgewood that time, we're having lunch, Geisel and some of the fellas. You hit him up for money."

"He didn't pay me for a job. I didn't know you were one of the people there."

The little man smiled a little smile. "Geisel, he was embarrassed. You put the blocks to him right there, people watching."

"I needed the money."

The smile went away. He looked at me again, still as a lizard. "I want you to do something for me."

"OK."

"If you hear from Leonard Geisel, I want you should phone this number." He wrote it on a piece of paper, the scratching of the fountain pen etching the background thrumming sound in the room. I looked at it and put it in my pocket.

"OK."

He opened a desk drawer, took out a number ten envelope and handed it to me. There was money inside, a thick conscience-stopping wad of it.

"For your trouble," he said.

Refusing the cash would have been dumb. "Thank you," I said and stood up.

"The helicopter will fly you back."

"Thank you."

I ceased to exist, and his attention went back to the ledger. I got up and opened the door.

"Mr. Rafferty."

"Yes?" I turned, but he did not lift his eyes from his accounting.

"Don't lose that number."

Five

I CLOSED THE DOOR ON the little man's room and heard an odd metallic clicking sound. My hand was trembling so much that the ring on my right hand was vibrating against the doorknob. Delayed shock, I thought, letting out a long shivery breath and putting my hands in my pockets.

I looked around the laundry for Lou Savelek. I didn't really want to see him; I just felt like asking him who was going to clean up the mess waiting for me at home. But Lou was gone.

The van was still there, parked in the loading block, the driver behind the wheel. He was middle-aged, pot-bellied, with a 1950s haircut over a face that had fallen in upon itself. He turned to me as I got into the passenger seat and said, "Where?"

"Back to the airport."

He put the van in gear and drove with methodical precision to the south terminal. The helicopter was where we'd left it, rotors turning slowly as the motor idled, the over-size pilot anonymous behind mirror shades. Thirty-five minutes later we swung in from the sea over Canadian Forces Base Comox, passed the battle-grey Aurora sub-chasers parked on the tarmac and angled down to the lit-tle civilian terminal squeezed up against the west side of the air base. Another fifteen minutes and I was getting out of a cab and climbing my front steps.

There was a Loomis envelope in the mailbox. I tore it open and scanned its contents. It contained an open-ended return ticket on a small local airline's flight to Sechelt across the Strait of Georgia. The date of the flight was today. There were also five hundred dollars in cash and a note from Karen: "Miggs will have someone meet you," fol-lowed by her stylized letter K. No "Dear Sid." No "Love, Karen."

I went inside, kicking aside debris, heading for the kitchen. Tea leaves were still spread over the counter, and I scooped them by hand into the pot, boiled water and made myself a cup of restorative. It smelled sweet and musty, like a warm hiding place.

I took the tea into the living room, turned the couch back upright, replaced one of its seat cushions and sat down. The flight time on the ticket gave me a few hours to kill, and I briefly thought about cleaning up. Then I sipped my tea and thought about nothing much.

After a while I noticed that I had finished the tea. I wanted a second cup, but the kitchen seemed a hell of a long way to go. I closed my eyes and tried counting the aches I had acquired in my visit to High Country Mining and my excursion with Lou Savelek.

I decided that this was not an ordinary week, and it was OK for me to feel a little used up. I also deserved a little luxury. I would call somebody and hire them to come over and straighten up the mess that surrounded me.

I looked around for the phone but couldn't see it amidst the rubble. So I started from the wall socket where the cord jacked in and followed the beige wire, tugging until I turned up my combination telephone and answering machine under an overturned armchair and a pile of paperbacks.

The way I saw it, Lou's employers wanted to find the Weasel, and probably for a good reason. So Lou had turned over my place, then hauled me off to Vancouver to see if I could be of any assistance.

I wondered if they had tapped my phone. I unscrewed the mouthpiece, and nothing fell out. Was that a good sign? I considered taking the base plate off the phone but I wouldn't know a bug unless it had "bug" printed on it and even then I might be wrong.

"Well," I told the empty room, "the hell with Geisel and Savelek and all of them." I had two thousand bucks in the envelope the little man had given me plus the five hundred

Karen had sent; it was enough to put a smile on my banker's face and keep me in bread and jam for a while. I was out of the squeeze, my ex-wife had given me some interesting work to do and if I just put my head down and concentrated on the job at hand, I'd be able to forget how royally I'd screwed up my career and marriage.

I couldn't call the cleaning service because I couldn't find the phone book. Finally I drove over to a place I'd seen in Courtenay, gave them a spare key and a hundred-dollar bill. I told them the mess was somebody's idea of a joke and asked them to clean it up and leave the key in the tea caddy.

I went to the bank, put the rest of the cash into my account and thought I detected a crack in the manager's smooth face that might some day hatch into a smile. Then I drove home, changed into unwrinkled slacks and a sports jacket, packed a few things and threw them into the back of the Concord.

The package of bumf Geisel had sent me was still in the car. I picked it up.

"Dead job," I said. I tossed it into the plastic garbage can in the corner of the garage then put the container outside for the cleanup crew to dispose of. The can was jammed full, but the weekly pickup would be today or tomorrow.

I got to the airport fifteen minutes before the plane to Sechelt would load and leave. I checked in at the ticket desk and sat in the little waiting area that overlooked the parking lot.

A plain brown sedan pulled into a space in the area reserved for rental cars. The two men in the car did not get out but sat motionless in the front seat, their faces shadowed by the vehicle's sun visors. They seemed to be looking straight at me, and I fought down an urge to slide out of my seat and move away from the window. I'm paranoid, I thought. Couple of civil servants talking to each other in a rent-a-car, and I start to sweat.

The ticket agent called the flight to Sechelt. I put my keys and coins in the little basket and passed through the metal detector. I knew from experience that the wedding ring in my pants pocket was too small to ring any bells. I refilled my pockets, showed my ticket to the flight attendant at the exit door and walked to the waiting Dash 7 turboprop.

I took a window seat looking out on the terminal. I could see my old car parked in the overnight area. For the first time I noticed that the explosion had left dark streaks on its battered paint.

More character, I thought. *In fact, any more character and it will be about ready for the wreckers.*

The plane's engines whined and we began to trundle toward the runway. I looked back at my car again. A man was leaning on it, looking into the back window. Then the plane angled onto a taxiway and I couldn't see anymore.

Don't let anybody steal my car, I prayed to whoever is the patron saint of distressed writers. *I don't have any theft insurance.* Sechelt is scarcely twenty minutes across Georgia Strait from Comox. There was only enough time for the flight attendants to distribute complimentary candies before we were gliding down to the resort town's tiny airport. I had kept my battered carryall with me on the plane, so I had nothing to wait for. I crossed the tarmac and went inside.

The terminal building was spartan: one small room with a ticket counter, some plastic chairs and a wooden shelf on which baggage was set for pickup. The few others who had gotten off the plane with me filtered through, picked up bags, exchanged hugs and greetings with friends and family and straggled out to the parking lot. The outbound passengers comprised a foursome of happy retirees on their way to Vancouver and probably thence to a cruise ship, and a mixed trio of business types — two men and a woman — checking in at the departures window.

I gave the terminal a 360-degree scan; nobody was holding up a cardboard sign with my name on it. But when I turned back to the counter, the two suits were heading for the security check-through, and the woman was right there in front of me.

She was about my age, tall, with red hair, short and swept somehow sideways, and a grownup girl-next-door face that framed the most disarming sea-green eyes I had ever seen.

She had on a green skirt and top combo that fitted her just the way it should. And she was wearing the warmest smile anybody had aimed my way in a long time. I could feel my mouth widening in a grin that had to be way up on Richter's goofiness scale. My cheek muscles were complaining about the unaccustomed stretching.

"Sid Rafferty?" she said. She had one of those throaty voices, the kind Suzanne Pleshette used to turn on Bob Newhart when he had a show worth watching. "I'm Maureen Migliorini. You can call me Mo."

She held out a hand. I took it and shook it but I couldn't seem to get any words ready on the firing line. Her eyebrows went up. "Are you OK?"

I couldn't remember the last time I had reacted so strongly on a first encounter. Finally I got the face muscles under control and could exercise enough presence of mind to stop working her hand. "I'm fine," I said. "Just fine, never better."

"Well ... fine," she said. "The car's outside. I'll take you over to the place."

I followed her. It was easy to do. She had the kind of figure they don't feature in *Vogue* magazine, solid and well packed, and she moved it well. She led me to a beat-up Hyundai sedan parked by the chain-link fence that contained the airfield. The two men she had been seeing off were about to board the Dash 7. They waved at her, and she flashed them a beacon of a smile before unlocking the car, getting in and reaching over to open the passenger door for me. My eyes followed every motion she made.

I tossed my bag into the back and buckled up while she steered us out of the parking area. "It's only a few minutes," she said.

I checked her ring finger; nothing there, but that doesn't mean much any more. "Are you his wife?" I asked.

She laughed. I liked the sound of it. "Sister. Tony's my little brother."

I liked the sound of that too. "You don't call him Miggs."

"No. But make sure you do. He doesn't like being Tony."

We were on the winding two-laner that hugs the Sunshine Coast from the northern tip of the Sechelt Peninsula down to the fishing village of Gibsons where CBC used to shoot the "Beachcombers" series. Roger Gambowsky had worked on that show. I told Mo that and asked if she'd known him.

"No. We're not local. Tony came here a few months ago to set up his place. I came to help." She swung out and passed a slow-moving car. "And to be somewhere I wouldn't run into my ex-husband or … never mind."

I indicated the car we had just passed. "That was an OMIAH," I said. I wasn't going to pry about the ex-husband or anything else. Maybe his worst fault was being nosy on short acquaintance.

She looked in the rear-view mirror. "What's an OMIAH?" she said.

I spelled it out. "Number two worst driving hazard," I told her. "Old Man In A Hat."

She tapped the steering wheel. "OK," she said. "I'll bite. What's number one?"

"OMIAHIAC," I said.

She waited.

"Old Man In A Hat In A Cadillac," I said.

"Tony ought to like you," she said.

I got the impression he did. Or at least he liked showing me around what he called the compound, which covered a few hectares between the highway and a low bluff overlooking a shingle beach. A network of boardwalks ran from one cabin to another and met at a low-slung main building. There were a couple of blacktopped basketball courts, an outdoor swimming pool and a corral in which a yearling deer ignored a pair of sheep. A carved wooden sign over the driveway told me the place was called Camp Second Chance.

Miggs motored from one attraction to the next in his power chair, pointing out this and that. Then he took me inside the big building, showed me the physio room, the whirlpool, the rec room and the lounge. Somewhere along the way Mo left us, saying something about returning a call. I watched her go.

Miggs and I ended up in what he called his study. It held a desk with no chair behind it, a state-of-the-art IBM PC and a lot of books on oak veneer shelves. I would have expected plenty of dare-to-be-great motivational stuff; instead it was an eclectic circus, everything from the dialogues of Plato to the dialogue of Elmore Leonard.

He wheeled his chair behind the desk and looked at me looking at his books.

"Quite a selection," I said.

"It was a phase I went through. I never had time to read before." He lifted one leg in his hands and let it fall. "But it's pretty weak beer." He slapped an arm of the chair. "This is the hard stuff. Real life. Sit down."

I moved a couple of books off a wooden chair and sat, took out my pen and notepad. Crossed my legs. Waited for him to speak. Uncrossed them and waited some more.

"So," I said.

"So what do you think?" he asked.

"I don't know where to start."

"Well, what do you think about the layout?" He waved toward the window, where the sky was darkening to evening. "I mean, this is just phase one. Eventually, I'm thinking all kinds of stuff: Olympic-quality training facility, horses for therapeutic riding, video-production facility. It'll be fantastic."

"I'm impressed."

"Great," he said. He laced his fingers behind his neck and leaned back in his power chair.

"But I guess I'm not making the connection."

"Connection. What connection?"

"Between all this and the political thing."

His hands slowly moved down to lie flat on the desk. "Why would there be a connection?"

"I don't know. I just assumed it must have had something to do with your running for the Socred leadership."

He became very still. "How do you know about that?"

I was beginning to feel as if I'd had this conversation before, not long before the door blew off a warehouse in Burnaby. "You do know why I'm here, don't you?"

"To look us over and see if we're eligible for funding by the Vancouver Foundation."

"I'm nothing to do with the Vancouver Foundation. I was sent here by Lyle Pastorel."

He didn't move or speak for several seconds. Then he yelled, "Mo! Hey, Mo!"

He had a loud voice. I jumped and he ducked his head in embarrassment. "Wo, sorry, man, didn't mean to scare you."

I retrieved my notepad from the floor. "It's OK."

Mo came in. She did an innocent smile to perfection. Miggs wasn't impressed. "You didn't introduce us all the way," he said. "I thought he was the Vancouver Foundation guy. Instead he's … "

"I'm the hack," I said.

"Yes, I know," said Mo.

"Well, I didn't know," said Miggs.

"That's because if I'd told you he was coming, you'd have been too busy to see him. Now you've got the whole afternoon free."

He shifted in his chair, looked out the window. "Well, maybe I don't. Maybe this is something you should be handling for me."

I started to stand up. "And maybe I should take a little walk," I said. But she put her hand on my shoulder and pressed me back into the chair. It was a warm hand.

"Don't move," she said. Tony looked like he wanted to be somewhere else. She leaned over his desk until they were nose to nose. "Listen," she said. "Sometimes you fish. Sometimes you cut bait. You're the one said you wanted to try politics, not me. So try it. Or drop it. But for God's sake, make up your mind!"

He could have been a kid caught raiding the cookie jar. He didn't do anything for a moment, then he shrugged. "OK, all right. Look, you guys go down, get some beers. I'll be there in a few minutes."

I had known women who would not have settled for the clean win, but Mo was not the kind to scour the battlefield, collecting trophies and taking scalps. She just turned to me and said, "Come on."

I followed her downstairs to the lounge. It was quiet except for the hum of the fridge behind the bar. "Beer OK, Sid?" she asked.

"Sure. And call me Raff."

"Raff," she said, seeing if she liked the sound of it. I knew I did.

She got us a couple of Granville Island lagers and steered me to a grouping of chairs, dark leather and black metal tubing. Mine sighed like a tired man when I lowered my weight into it. She sat across from me.

She sipped the beer and smiled. "Sorry," she said.

For that smile, I would have forgiven her if she'd hung me naked from a freeway overpass.

"No problem," I said.

"It's just that he'd have ducked and run if he'd known what you were here for."

"He change his mind about being in politics?"

She shrugged, looked out at the dark beyond the windows.

"Let me guess. He really doesn't want to be in politics. All he cares about is what he's trying to do with this place. The political thing is just to get publicity and maybe some loose money for the cause."

She swung those amazing eyes back to me, and I felt a

kind of vertigo as if I were actually being pulled forward into the greenness.

I was staring at her. "Are you all right?" she asked.

"Not for a while," I said. "But I think I might be getting better."

Miggs rolled in, and she stretched out a foot to push a chair out of his way.

"Look," he said, "about, you know … "

"Skip it, he's already figured it out," said Mo.

"Oh," he said and did the cookie-jar face again. I bet he had done pretty well with the kind of women who liked to play mom. "Well, I guess that's that," he said.

My turn to shrug.

Mo put down her beer. "I'm sorry we took up your time, Raff," she said. "I'll find you a bunk for tonight and drive you back to the airport in the morning."

She stood up. Miggs wheeled his chair in a half-turn. The motor was loud in the stillness.

"Hold it," I said. "Let's talk."

So we talked, got some more beers and talked some more as night came down. They told me about their plans for the compound. I told them about Karen and Pastorel, about the peculiar relationship.

"Upshot is this," I said, "I don't owe Pastorel any favours. You're not trying to rip anybody off so you can put the money in your own pocket. The people who are footing the bill are trying to buy themselves a government. As far as they're concerned this is high-risk capital, so they're not going to get too sweaty about the project going wonky. More important," and I said this right to those pools of green, "I like you guys. You're trying to do something good here. I'll play along."

Miggs did a little side-to-side thing with the wheelchair that was some kind of end-zone victory dance. Mo gave me a smile I would have traded heaven for.

"What do you say we start first thing tomorrow?" she said.

"Suits me," said Miggs. He yawned and stretched, said, "I'm going to bed," and wheeled himself out.

Mo said she wanted another beer. When she looked at me, I said, "Sure."

She came back with the bottles and took a chair beside me. "Anything more you want to tell me?" she said.

"Where to begin?" I said. I told her things I had never told anybody before: about Ottawa and the twins, about the movie deal and the screwups. She listened well, didn't ask many questions.

Something was growing between us. It wasn't just that I felt I could tell her things that hurt; I *wanted* to tell her those things. Some men play for a woman's pity; most men would rather be blowtorched than let a vulnerability see the light of day. I'd always leaned toward the tough-guy act, but some quality of Mo's slipped right under the shell and effortlessly drew out the pink, unprotected meat.

Eventually I ran out of things to say. We just sat there, nodding to the rhythm of the fridge's motor. She was looking at her hands, the long, strong fingers folded around the empty bottle, while she thoughtfully chewed the inside of her lip.

Then she looked at me, long and level, and I had the impression she was making up her mind. She stood up. "Come on," she said. "We'll find you a place to sleep."

The air outside was sweet and soft, one of those nights Ray Bradbury used to write about when I was a kid, with just a hint of colour left in the west and the stars like snow crystals melting on warm black satin. The sheep were hunkered down in their pen, mumbling to each other about the deer.

She led me to a cabin that would sleep four. It was a small cozy room with polished log walls and beige carpet, and except for the extra-wide door and the handrails on the beds, it could have been in a classy summer camp for rich kids.

The mattresses were bare. "I'll get you some bedding," she said and went out.

After four beers I needed the bathroom. I washed up, found no towels and had to dry my hands and face on my shirt. The mirror over the sink said I was still slipping into the goofy grin. I experimented with some other expressions, but my face kept defaulting back to goofiness.

I was humming "Stranger in Paradise" as I went back into the main room. She'd made up the bed but she hadn't left. She was sitting on the thermal blanket, hands folded on her knees, like a schoolgirl working out the answer to a classroom question in her head.

She looked up at me and sighed. "I want you to know, this is not the kind of thing I do." Then she stood up and pulled back the covers. "Get in."

There are moments when a sensible man says nothing and does what he's told. This was clearly one of those moments, and I was just as clearly not a sensible man.

"I don't want you feeling sorry for me," I said.

"Sorry doesn't come into it," she said. "I don't know what I feel for you, except that there's one hell of an attraction, and I'm thinking just once in my life I ought to dive in and see what happens. Now get in the bed."

She went into the bathroom and closed the door. I heard water running, then a faint "Damn," as she discovered the lack of towels. I stripped and got under the covers. The sheets were smooth and icy, but that wasn't why I was shivering.

The light went out under the bathroom door, leaving the cabin lit only by the faintest glow filtering past the curtains from the main building.

About a million years went by. I knew she was standing there behind the closed bathroom door and I hoped she wasn't going to change her mind. Then the door opened, I heard the whisper of her bare feet on the carpet and she was there beside me.

"Hi," I said eloquently.

"Just hold me for a minute," she said. I put my arms around her, buried my face in her hair that smelled like exotic fruit. Her breath tickled my shoulder with puffs of warmth.

"This isn't me," she said. "I've always been careful. I organize things; I don't jump into them."

I stroked her back. "I don't want you to do anything that'll make you feel bad," I said, and even as I said it, a part of me silently commented on how the same statement could simultaneously be completely true and completely false.

"You can't always be careful," she said. She ran her hands up and down my spine and drew me closer, her skin like a hot shock wave against my chest and belly.

I stroked her lower back. "I haven't done this in a long time," I said.

She slid a thigh over mine. "Me neither."

I swallowed. "Maybe we should take it slow."

"Like hell," she said, and kissed me and pulled me onto her.

I fell into her, and it was everything it was supposed to be but had never been before. She was lithe and strong, smooth as heavy cream, and at her centre was a wet swirling heat that swallowed me and lifted me and had me gasping words I couldn't remember while she bit my shoulder and shuddered and called me her lovely man.

We lay breathing together, saying nothing, and she slept against me. But I couldn't lie with her and not touch her, and when I did she awoke. Then we found each other, slow and sure this time, and we went up together and came down together, and all was finally all right.

She wasn't there when I woke up, just the smell of her hair on the pillow. I went looking for her and found her in a sunlit room, laying three places for breakfast but only two chairs — Miggs brought his own.

It was a little difficult, sitting across from each other, not sure what to do with our hands or our eyes, while Miggs filled awkward pauses with reminiscences of his firefighting days and snippets of his dreams for the rehab centre. But we got through it somehow. Then Miggs said he was going for his morning workout, so she and I walked through the grounds to where the bluff looked west over the sea. The onshore breeze was soft and salty. She picked up a twig and threw it down to the sand.

"It was pretty awful of me, just jumping on you like that," she said.

"I thought you were wonderful."

"It's not the kind of thing I do."

I took her hand. I could feel a pulse but I didn't know whether it was mine or hers. "I'm glad you don't. I wouldn't want to think that the woman I'm falling in love with goes around jumping on strange men."

She smiled at me, and I realized I might spend a lot of my future time thinking up lines that would win me that smile. "You're not that strange," she said.

"You don't really know me yet."

The smile went away. "I'd like to."

"OK. Give me the forms, I'll fill them in."

She put her arm around my waist. "One thing," she said. "Don't try too hard. This is either going to work out just fine on its own or it's not. OK?"

I put my arm around her and we walked back toward the buildings. "OK."

Way back in the Saturday matinées of my childhood, Randolph Scott would always spot the bad guys lying in ambush by a telltale glint of sunlight off their silver hat brims or rifle barrels. Now I found out that it happened in real life too.

"There's somebody underneath the bushes over there, watching us," I whispered. "Don't look."

On the inland side of Miggs's property, between the highway and his well-trimmed lawns, was a thick bramble of blackberry bushes, the kind of volunteer hedge that will throw itself up just about anywhere on the British Columbia south coast. Someone had wriggled under the thorns and was tracking us through some kind of scope. The sun glinted again on the glass.

"This ex-husband, he's not some loony who follows you around, is he?" I asked Mo.

She made a face. "My ex didn't pay any attention to me when we were together, much less now. Last I heard he was still chasing teenagers."

We walked over to a cabin with a front door facing the hidden observer. I asked her to hang around outside as if she were waiting for me to come right back out.

"I hope you're not trying to impress me," she said. "Nothing impresses me less than people trying to impress me."

"Hah hah," I said. Then, because she looked worried, I put away the comic side of my nature and assured her that I would not do anything stupid. "I'm mostly just curious," I said.

I went into the cabin. I shut the door, crossed the small room, opened a window that faced the sea and crawled out. I ran straight for the bluffs and slid down to the beach, scuttled south for a couple of hundred metres then turned back inland along a dry stream bed.

The watercourse meandered through a patch of scrub spruce and hemlock that extended right up to the road, where it led into a culvert. Crouched down, I crossed under the two-lane highway and emerged into the ditch on the other side. Staying low, I went north until I was directly across the road from the spot where the hidden observer lay beneath the hedge.

From this angle he was not so hidden. The brambles were less than a couple of metres deep, and from under the thorns emerged a pair of denim pant legs that produced two thin ankles which ended in small-sized hush puppies. He was lying belly down.

I crossed the road and stood looking down at his worn heels and scuffed soles. His right foot was twitching nervously as he watched Mo and waited for me to come out of the cabin.

Maybe it was all the stress and pain of the past few weeks. Maybe it was because this guy was horning in on the nicest thing that had happened to me in a long time. Maybe it was just because the feet were small and the ankles were skinny, but I grabbed those ankles and yanked hard.

It was the first time I had laid violent hands upon another human being since my last schoolyard fight, and it felt disturbingly good. The man didn't weigh much and he came out from under the hedge fast and squawking; being pulled through the thorns had left blood tracks along the back of his neck and hands. I let go of his ankles and he rolled over, pulling his knees up to his chest, where he clutched what looked to me like an expensive video camera.

It seemed to be a professional's rig, longer and bulkier than a home video camcorder, with a fabric-covered microphone extending from the middle of a concave dish the size of a saucepan lid.

"The hell you think you're doing?" I said. I felt like kicking him.

He didn't say anything, just stared back with hard dark eyes. Then he unfolded himself and got to his feet, pulled a thorn from his nylon jacket and turned to walk away.

I put a hand on his arm. "Whoa, buddy, hold it right there," I said, but he shook off my grip and walked on faster. That was when I recognized him. He was the man who had taken my picture on Georgia Street and disappeared into the crowd around the old courthouse fountain.

"Wait a minute," I said. He didn't wait, and I had to trot to catch him up. That felt silly, and feeling silly cancelled out any hope I had of playing tough guy.

I pursued him like an ineffectual ghost trying to haunt a skeptic. We were quickstepping up the soft shoulder of the highway now, toward a beat-up Volkswagen bus parked under some trees north of Miggs's property. The man looked straight ahead and kept moving.

We reached the VW. The man threw open the sliding door. Inside was the camera's carrying case, with moulded foam supports for the equipment. He began to stow the camera away, still not acknowledging my existence. He closed the case, then went to slide the door shut.

"Hell with this," I said and caught the door with the heel of my hand. I reached in, popped open the carrying case, grabbed the video camera and backed away.

That got his attention. "Hey!" he bleated and went for it, but I had already found how to open the side hatch and get what I wanted. I pushed the camera back into his arms but I held onto the videotape.

I reached around behind me and tucked the tape into the back of my belt, then balled my fists and said, "You want it, come and get it."

I don't believe I had ever seen anyone look at me with sheer hatred before. It was like being hit by a wave of cold energy. I thought, *This guy better not have a gun in that bus,* but then he turned away and it was as if I didn't exist again. He stowed the camera in the vehicle, climbed behind the wheel and sped off. I memorized the licence number.

I heard a scuff of gravel and turned to see Mo running up the highway toward me. "Everything's fine," I said.

She watched the VW out of sight along the curving road. "Who was he? What did he want?"

"He was taking pictures, video." I showed her the tape.

"Well, let's take a look at it."

"We should tell your brother."

Miggs had finished his laps in the pool and was working out with hand weights in the physio room. From the waist up, shirtless, he looked like he was carved from hardwood. With or without legs, I wouldn't want him to be mad at me.

The observer's description rang no bells for Miggs. And he had no idea why anyone should be watching us.

"Could he be an insurance spy, trying to get evidence that you're not really injured?" I wondered.

"Yeah, right," said Miggs, lifting a formless leg in both hands and letting it slap against the wheelchair seat. "Nah. They do that before they settle, not after."

I told them about seeing the man in downtown Vancouver, how he had taken my picture.

"Maybe it's not you he was spying on," I said. "Maybe it's me."

"OK," said Mo, "say it's you. So why is he interested in you?"

I thought about it. Nothing came. "Let's take a look at the tape," I suggested.

We went over to the lounge and popped the tape into the VCR. I pressed play and got nothing but snow. "It's blank," I said.

"Press rewind," said Mo. "Let's see what he shot before you tackled him."

"I never said I was technically apt," I said and rewound the tape.

There were only a few minutes of raw footage. An establishing shot of the sign over the driveway taken from the road. Another from a different angle. A shot of Mo and me walking toward the beach, then heading back toward the camera.

The long-range directional mike hadn't worked too well. The soundtrack just gave disconnected snippets of our conversation and had even missed the part where I'd said there was somebody in the bushes.

Miggs said, "Run it again." He watched his sister and me put our arms around each other. "Anything I should know?" he asked Mo.

"No," she said and held up a finger to me. "Don't say anything. He teases."

I cleared my throat. "Well, the tape doesn't tell us much about our spy," I said.

"It tells us he's an amateur," said Mo. "That's not professional-quality footage. I think we can assume he's not a reporter."

I shrugged. "Then we're still in the dark."

Miggs rubbed his nose. "You said you got a licence plate."

I nodded.

"Let me have it."

I told him the plate number, and he wheeled over to the phone.

In American movies, private eyes and other civilians are always calling friends in the police department and getting them to run licence plates. In British Columbia most local police forces are RCMP, and the RCMP does not run plates for anyone.

But some cities like Vancouver have their own police forces, some of whose members are not quite as by-the-book as the Mounties. Miggs had a friend who was a corporal on the Vancouver force; they'd volunteered together on the North Shore rescue team.

Miggs's friend said he would run the plate and get back to him.

"Just like Dennis Becker," I said.

"Who?" said Miggs. I couldn't believe he'd never seen the "Rockford Files."

After that we got down to the work I'd been hired to do. I spent a couple of hours prying personal background and philosophical inclinations out of Tony Migliorini. The personal stuff wasn't too hard; Miggs had nothing to hide.

The philosophical material was more difficult. Like most Canadians, Miggs thought politics was a game played by and for politicians. The idea that there might be a foundation

of principle under the ploys and posturings had not occurred
to him.

He didn't know whether he was left-wing or right-
wing. He was in favour of free enterprise (the catch-all
slogan of the Social Credit Party) but he also wanted a government that cared about the disadvantaged (the thumbnail
description of the NDP).

In the end we decided that he was a naive populist who
would be comfortable with middle-of-the-road economic and social policies. Besides, the people who wanted him
to be Socred leader didn't want him for his political ideas;
they wanted him for his personal popularity.

Fitting him into the Social Credit world view would not
be too hard. The party had always enjoyed a remarkably
flexible ideology. On the one hand it stood foursquare for
private enterprise and against big government. But W.A.C.
Bennett had had no trouble reaching out with the other
hand to nationalize the province's private electric utility, a
railroad and the ferry fleet.

When Dave Barrett's NDP were briefly in power in the
early 1970s, they had established a government monopoly
in car insurance. In 1975 Bill Bennett's triumphant Socreds
made loud noises about free enterprise as they chased the
social democrats back into the opposition benches — but
they kept the auto insurance in government hands, turning
it into a useful cash cow for the provincial coffers.

The Socreds were known for the flexibility of their political principles. I'd once written a line for a politician's roast that summed up the party spectrum in British Columbia: the Tories stand for big business; the NDP stands for big labour; Liberals will stand for just about anything; and the Socreds stand for election.

I borrowed Miggs's word processor and spent the afternoon drafting him a short biography and a statement of principles. I called the first one "Who I Am" and the second "Where I Stand." If they weren't Churchillian rhetoric, they were reasonably serviceable prose.

Miggs and Mo read them. "You're really quite good at this," Mo said.

"Thanks."

Miggs felt a little funny about seeing himself all laid out in politician's language. But he went along. "Now what happens?" he wanted to know.

"I send it over to Pastorel, and he'll probably want to tinker with it, add in whatever trigger words the latest polls say will make hearts flutter among the party rank and file." I shrugged. "I don't know what his strategy will be. He'll be in touch."

"OK," he said. "Well, I gotta do some things." And he wheeled out of the lounge, leaving Mo and me to figure out what we were going to do next.

"I don't have to go," I said.

"I think it would be better if you did."

My face must have betrayed me, because she touched her hand to my cheek and smiled. "I just want to think about things. But you're doing fine."

"What about the weirdo in the bushes? He might be back."

"I don't think so. He didn't act too brave."

Miggs's cop friend hadn't called back while we were working. When Miggs had tried to reach him during the afternoon, he was told the corporal was testifying in court.

"It'll be OK," she said. "Call me in a couple of days. We'll talk."

"I'll look forward to it."

"Me too." And she flashed me that smile again.

So I kissed her and went and got my stuff together. She gave me a ride to the airport, and we kissed again in the parking lot. Then she drove away.

The plane for Comox left a half-hour later. I looked down at the Sunshine Coast falling away behind the vibrating wing and thought about her. I was a little scared but I was also happier than I'd been in a long, long time.

I collected my Concord from the Comox airport parking lot and rumbled down Pritchard Road into town. The sun was doing a nice job of setting. Roy Orbison was singing "In Dreams" on the oldies station, and I sang along until I got to the part that always makes my throat hurt.

I let myself into the house and found the living room spotless. The cleaning crew must have included some over-achievers; someone had sorted all my paperbacks alphabet-ically by authors' names.

The house felt different, peculiarly cozy. For the first time it was a place to come home to, a place to bring some-one home to. I went into the kitchen and put on the ket-tle for a pot of tea. While the water was heating, I went to the room I used as an office and faxed Miggs's bio and statement to Karen at Pastorel's.

The kettle squeaked at me, and I made the tea, then stood looking out the window at the mist playing over the moun-tains until it was brewed. I poured a cup and took it into the living room, stretched out on the couch and sipped. I let my mind go back to the night before, breakfast, the morning walk to the beach.

There was a dream I sometimes had — not a recurring dream that repeated itself exactly but a familiar motif that came up out of my unconscious every now and then. I would be in a house I knew well, maybe one of the places where I'd lived as a child, and suddenly I would find a door or a staircase that led into a series of rooms I hadn't known were there. There was no treasure in the secret rooms, no monster lurking. But somehow it felt good to find all the added space.

Sitting in my tidy home, my books neatly arranged,

sipping tea and looking back on the past twenty-four hours, I felt like I'd come across some extra rooms. I felt good. I felt as if there was a future again.

The doorbell rang.

I opened the door to find Conroy, the Coordinated Law Enforcement Unit cop, looking down at me. "Mr. Rafferty," he said. "I'd like to ask you a question."

I was too surprised to play any games. "Ask away," I said.

He didn't wait to be invited in. He brushed past me and took a long look around my pristine living room. Finally he turned and said, "Why does Leonard Geisel keep trying to get you on the phone?"

Six

"I DON'T UNDERSTAND," I SAID.

Conroy looked around for somewhere to sit and decided that my patchy old armchair would suit him best. He waved off my lukewarm gesture toward offering him a cup of tea. "Neither do I," he said. He looked at a notebook. "You said that you and Mr. Geisel were not friends, that it was just a business relationship."

"Yes."

"Then why does he keep trying to call you?"

My brain was starting to turn over again. "How would you know if he keeps trying to call me? Are you tapping my phone?" Suddenly my neat little home didn't feel so snug. It was as if the walls had turned out to be made of cheesecloth and wax paper.

Conroy did not answer.

"Listen," I said. "I'm willing to co-operate but I'm not going to be run through the mill. I haven't broken any laws, have I?"

He gave me the deadpan cop look. "Not that we know of."

"Am I the subject of an investigation?"

"You're starting to sound like a lawyer, Mr. Rafferty."

I had had enough. I'd liked my life so much just a few minutes ago and I was not enjoying Conroy's injection of a little Kafka. "Funny thing is," I told him, "I'm not a lawyer but I know quite a few of them — including my old boss, who used to be the federal minister of justice. And who happens to be a senator in Ottawa. I'm thinking maybe I should get in touch with him, just to make sure I'm covered. Or maybe you'd like to answer the question I just asked and you just ducked."

Conroy sucked his lips into his teeth, watching me, weighing something up. He came to a decision. "No," he said, "you are not the subject of an investigation. And no, we are not tapping your phone. Now why is he trying to call you?"

I looked over at the phone. The message-received light was not flashing. "I don't know," I said.

"Do you know where he is?"

"No."

Conroy looked the way a potato would look if it was not happy. I waited to see what he would do.

The phone rang. "Excuse me," I said. "If this is him, you can ask him yourself." I answered it.

It wasn't the Weasel; it was Miggs. His buddy the Vancouver police corporal had come through with the licence plate number. The VW bus was registered to a Nestor Gilfillan, with an address in the sprawling Vancouver suburb of Surrey.

I turned my back on Conroy and wrote down the name and address on a pad. That didn't do any good. Conroy stood up and read what I'd written over my shoulder. Then he jotted down the name in his notebook and sat down again.

"Does that name mean anything to you?" I asked Miggs. Nestor Gilfillan's name meant nothing to either of us. I thanked Miggs, told him I couldn't talk and got off the line.

"What does the name Nestor Gilfillan mean to you?" Conroy asked.

"Nothing," I said. "And you know, Mr. Conroy, I don't think I'm going to answer any more questions. In fact I don't like you coming in here and invading my privacy. I haven't broken any laws that I know of and I think you're lying to me about tapping my phone."

I was getting angry. It doesn't happen very often and it doesn't last long, but it seemed to me that I'd had about enough of everybody — bankers, clients, cops, thugs, mysterious mining guys and Nestor Gilfillan with his video camera — and I just wanted these people out of my life.

Conroy smoothed down his comb-over and chewed his inner lip some more. "Tell you what," he said. "I don't want you to go into a big fuss about your phone. I said we're not tapping it and we're not. We'd need a judge's warrant and we don't have probable cause to get a warrant. A guy like you, used to work for the justice minister, you ought to know that."

Now that I thought about it, I did know that. Back when I'd been writing ministerial speeches about law reform, the whole question of wiretaps and surveillance had been under my minister's mandate, and he had put through Parliament the stringent rules that now applied. It was not something I'd thought about since.

"Geisel has a cellular," Conroy continued, "and let's just say we happen to know his frequency. So every time he makes a call or tries to make a call, he's going out on the public airwaves. Nobody's privacy is getting invaded; anybody can pick it up on a scanner. It so happens the only calls he's making are to your number."

"I see," I said. I didn't see at all. But I wasn't feeling so mad anymore.

"The reason I'm telling you this is 'cause I have a feeling there is something you want to tell me."

"What do you mean?"

"Call it cop's instinct." He looked at his notebook. "Is it maybe something to do with this Nestor Gilfillan?"

"I don't know anything about Nestor Gilfillan."

"Would you like to?" he asked.

I sat down. "What's going on here?" I said.

"Mr. Rafferty, I think we're about to trade some secrets. Just to show willing, I'll go first. Nestor Gilfillan. He's a small-time private detective, works out of an office in his garage. In the old days he'd have been eyeballing motel rooms through keyholes to get evidence for divorce cases. Nowadays I think he does insurance surveillance, employee background checks, that kind of thing."

"Why would he be interested in me?"

"I don't know. Is he?"

I shook my head. "I don't get it. What's he got to do with CLEU?"

Conroy spread his hands. "Nothing. I knew him from back when I was on the Vancouver force. He's one of those guys likes to hang around places cops go after work; probably wanted to be a cop but flunked the interview or something. Or probably the physical — he's pretty much a shrimp."

I thought about what Conroy was telling me. It still didn't add up. The only angle I could see was that somebody in an insurance company might suspect Miggs of not being paralysed. But that was dumb and it didn't explain why Gilfillan had snapped my picture days before I'd even met the Migliorinis.

Conroy waited while I mulled the information over. "So?" he said.

"So nothing," I told him. "It doesn't fit. I'm not involved in any insurance cases. I haven't applied for any sensitive jobs." An idea occurred to me. "Is he connected with any political movements that you know of?"

"Nah." He smoothed his comb-over. "I think his wife might have been but I don't really remember."

"Then I'm blank," I said.

"Sorry the information doesn't help," Conroy said. "But now it's your turn." He waited.

I thought about it. Whatever was happening with Geisel and the little man in the back room of the laundry, I was not a part of it. Even though I'd taken the money in the envelope, I was just a bystander.

"I'm just a bystander," I said. And then I told him about coming home and finding my place tossed. I told about Lou Savelek and the helicopter ride and Uncle Enzo with the corpse's eyes. I didn't mention the money but I told him they had scared me.

"I don't think you need to be scared if you're just a bystander," Conroy said. "You are not the only person they've been talking to. They want to see Geisel."

"Why?" I asked.

"We don't know," Conroy said, and it sounded like the truth. "When they got interested, we got interested."

"Does it have anything to do with that explosion? Was that some kind of mob thing?"

"You've been watching too much TV," Conroy said. "As far as we know, there's no connection. Those two guys," — he flipped through his notebook and found the page — "Byfield and Polowicz, they were just a couple of American mining engineers with good international credentials. They had chemicals of some kind stored in bins and it looked like somebody was smoking where he shouldn't have been. There was no bomb."

He asked me a couple of questions, details about my trip to the laundry. I answered truthfully. He put his notebook away and stood up.

"Well, Mr. Rafferty," he said, "my advice is you should keep on just being a bystander. If Leonard Geisel calls you, I'd like you to tell him to get in touch with me. If he doesn't want to do that, I would like you to call me. And I would advise you to keep some distance between you and him."

"That's probably good advice," I said.

"There is no probably about it."

He left, and I got myself another cup of tea. I wondered why Geisel would be calling me. I wondered why Gilfillan wanted pictures of me. But mainly I wondered when I would see Maureen Migliorini again.

The fax machine beeped. I went into the office and found a note from Karen. "Got material. Looks good. Can you come over for workshop session tomorrow afternoon?" Again no salutation, no warm words above the stylized K. But it didn't bother me. I faxed her back a note saying I'd be over right after lunch.

It was getting on to supper time, and a quick scan of the kitchen cupboards revealed that it had been a while since I went shopping.

I drove down to Portuguese Joe's, a fish store with its front door on the Dyke Road and its back to the river. A big flock of gulls, a squad of crows and a couple of bald eagles were wheeling around over the little wharf out back. The noise was like something out of Hitchcock's movie. I bought a quarter-kilo of shrimp and scallops that had been plucked from Georgia Strait not more than twelve hours earlier and paid the kind of price that makes city folk turn green.

Then I went back up the hill to Comox and followed the main drag to the SuperValu. There I picked up some red and green peppers, snow peas, mushrooms and a bag of no-name noodles. I added a jar of hot and spicy plum sauce. May, my favourite cashier, was at the express check-out. She was a small-town goddess with a wry sense of humour, and I flirted with her as if we were teenagers — or at least the way I would have flirted as a teenager if I hadn't spent the years from fourteen to nineteen as a tongue-tied, pimply gawk.

I stopped by the beer and wine store for a bottle of chilled liebfraumilch and opened it as soon as I got home. I sipped while I stir-fried the veggies, boiled the noodles, sautéed the seafood in plum sauce, then mixed the whole thing together and dug in.

I ate in the living room so I could watch the news. I'd missed the local political stuff that usually led off the BCTV newscast now that the Vander Zalm regime was clashing its gears and giving off sparks in all directions; I could catch the update at eleven-thirty. There was nothing else of much interest except the incredible spectacle of three hundred thousand East Germans flooding through the streets of Leipzig and demanding that the city's government resign.

Four thousand East Germans had been holed up at the West German embassy in Prague, and now the Communists had agreed to grant them exit visas so they could go west. Thousands more were pouring through Hungary into Austria. The Hungarians had torn down the barbed wire on the border. They were opting out of the cold war, and the Russians weren't saying whatever is Russian for boo. It looked as if Eastern Europe was alive with Germans in little four-wheeled smoke-pots that seemed to run mainly on motor oil. If this kept up, they'd be pouring over the Berlin Wall before Christmas.

I toasted the East Germans with West German wine and

switched the TV off, took my plate into the kitchen and washed up at the sink. Dusk was empurpling the mountains in a tourist-pleasing way. I could see the lights at Coronado below the clearcut ski slopes.

It was a beautiful place to live, and it looked like I'd be staying. I wondered if Mo would consider moving over.

I was out the door by seven a.m., burning down the Island Highway with the morning sun in my eyes and my ears full of earnest CBC radio news items. Social Credit's internal contortions were providing rich veins for commentators and political analysts to mine.

As the Socreds headed into their annual convention, there was hot debate over a proposal to remove from the party constitution a clause that committed them to follow Christian principles. A prominent Jewish ex-candidate named Michael Levy wanted to bring the issue to the floor. Fearing the prospect of a nasty floor-fight that would tear the already weakened party into religious and ethnic scraps, the provincial executive arranged for a nondebatable tabling motion to get the issue off the agenda.

But nobody bothered to tell Levy that the party brass were giving his issue a premature procedural burial. When he tried to speak on his motion, he was ruled out of order, then howled out of the room by the triumphant Zalmoids.

It made for great TV but it sent to hell the Socreds' hopes of looking like a real political party.

The damage was compounded manifold the next day, when the premier and some of his ministers told ethnic jokes at a supposedly off-the-record breakfast with convention delegates. Offended anti-Zalm Socreds walked away from their pancakes and right into the mikes and cameras of the waiting media, where they repeated the scurrilous lines and demanded apologies from their hapless boss.

I had to laugh. It seemed that the Socreds had contracted the traditional Tory mania for forming circular firing squads.

My interest was mainly pecuniary. As long as the governing party was chewing at its own innards, there would be paid work for people like me. I switched over to the oldies station and for the umpteenth time wondered who the hell Patty Herve was and why — if she had really been a Canadian rock-and-roll queen of the 1960s — I had never heard of her.

The nine o'clock ferry had me into Horseshoe Bay before eleven, and by the time the giant airhorns atop the old BC Hydro Building blasted out the first four notes of "O Canada" at noon, I was at a window table in my favourite restaurant. It was a little street-level place on Bute just down from Robson that made Breton-style crepes, including a chestnut-cream dessert number that I never got tired of.

To me the place felt like the old Vancouver, before corporate egotism turned the town's core into yet another cloned megacity of the 1980s. A pedestrian suddenly struck by amnesia on a downtown street of the new Vancouver might have to wander for blocks before a glimpse of mountains or sea between the anonymous glass towers would give a clue that this was not Akron or Pittsburgh.

That was not a problem in Lyle Pastorel's suite of offices, however, with its wide-angle view of the Lions Gate Bridge rising out of the trees of Stanley Park and arching across First Narrows to the North Shore. Those who could afford to place themselves above the common herd could always tell at a glance where they were.

His perfect receptionist showed me to a corner conference room done in teak and beige. There was coffee on a credenza, so I poured myself a cup, sat at one end of the big table and looked out the window until Karen came in. She was in pale green silk under a linen jacket. She took a seat around the corner of the table from me, neatly arranging a stack of papers in front of her.

"You look good," she said.

"I'm all right," I said.

"Are you staying in town?"

"No plans. Why?"

"It's a professional day tomorrow. No school. You could take the boys somewhere."

"I'd like that."

We smiled at each other, and it wasn't a stretch for me. I wanted to say something to her and I was still searching for the right opening when Lyle Pastorel entered at the head of a pack of suits.

A couple of them were familiar faces from the public-relations community, both of them considered heavy hitters. Lloyd Mackenzie was a veep for corporate communications at one of the big forest companies; Bas Cowper was from the industrial association that represented mining interests.

But then the total net worth of the room's occupants went up by an order of magnitude when Fritz Gershom walked in. He was a key playmaker on the VSE, a man who bought and sold companies as if they were commodities contracts. His haircuts cost more than my suits. I'd never met him, but the sharp-featured face was familiar from a dozen TV interviews.

Gershom closed the door behind him, but it reopened almost immediately to admit another financial celeb. Silver-haired Walter Fornoy was less flamboyant than the Howe Street maven, less likely to seek the limelight, but he was one of the few people west of Bay Street who could put up a quarter for every one of Gershom's nickels.

"Sorry I had to miss lunch, guys," Fornoy said. "But,

Lyle, may I take it everything was settled as we discussed on the phone?"

Pastorel nodded. "We can talk about it later," he said.

"Let's sit down. You all know Karen." He gestured to indicate me. "This is Sid Rafferty, our writer."

Mackenzie and Cowper said "Hi, Raff," and Gershom offered his dry hand. Fornoy was already sitting down and opening a tooled leather notepad. He looked at his wafer-thin Cartier. "I've only got an hour," he said.

"That's fine, Walter," said Karen. "If we can just have your input and Fritz's for the broad strategic strokes, the rest of us can do the detailed layout after and send it to you for review." She turned to Pastorel. "Lyle, do you want to begin?"

He leaned forward and put his elbows on the table. The polished wood distorted the reflection of his too-pink face and bright yellow tie, making an image that wasn't pleasant to look at. But maybe I was just prejudiced.

"We all know the background," he began. And he succinctly laid out the political history of the past three years. He began with how, after three years of "restraint" — a code word for heavy cutbacks in government services and social programs — Bill Bennett's Socred government had been heading for a brick wall in 1986. Not even the hoopla of the first successful world's fair in years, Expo 86, could make the electorate warm to Bennett's too-well-cultivated hard-ass image and give him a third term.

The party had needed a popular successor, but there was no obvious heir apparent who could romp to victory in a happy, party-uniting convention. There were too many contenders, too many splits in the centre-right coalition that was Social Credit.

Grace McCarthy, the grande dame who had rebuilt the party almost single-handedly for the Bennetts after the 1972 defeat, had the old Socreds behind her. Brian Smith, won over by Bennett from the Tories, had most of the new Social Credit troops — federal Conservatives willing to coalesce at the provincial level with rival federal Liberals, if that's what it took to keep the NDP out of power. Then there was Bud Smith from Kamloops, a major backroom boy with a strong regional power base.

Behind these three heavyweights came a straggle of small-fry optimists who hoped to do what Joe Clark had done at the 1976 national Tory leadership convention: come up the middle as a compromise after the big boys and girls had ground against each other and gotten nowhere.

And then from out of deepest suburban Richmond, where he ran a struggling theme park called Fantasy Gardens, came the supposedly retired politician Bill Vander Zalm, one of that unique breed of political zanies with which British Columbia regularly astounds and delights Canadians on the far side of the Rockies. Vander Zalm had been mayor of Surrey in the early seventies, presiding over a particularly bizarre municipal circus. He had then run for the leadership of the provincial Liberal Party, campaigning on a promise to do horrible things to drug dealers. When the Liberals failed to warm to his concepts, he'd jumped on Bill Bennett's Social Credit revival train as it began to gather momentum.

Bennett had put him in charge of the welfare rolls, and the flamboyant ex-merchant of garden supplies immediately grabbed headlines by announcing that he'd cut off from the provincial dole any able-bodied recipient who wouldn't pick up a shovel. There were none too many shovel-wielding jobs to be had at the time, but the stunt made Vander Zalm the darling of the Socred coalition's furthest right. Shovels bearing his autograph became popular items at party fundraising auctions.

Vander Zalm eventually pushed his luck too far around the cabinet table. Bennett moved him into the municipal affairs portfolio, where the ex-mayor crafted a bill that would have lifted the planning powers from every municipal hall in British Columbia and centralized them in Vander Zalm's office. Since the main job of municipal government is to manage land, passage of the planning bill would have left mayors and aldermen sitting around town halls with not much more to do than collect garbage and fill potholes. The minister, conversely, would have gained personal control over the zoning of every piece of property in the province.

Nobody but Vander Zalm thought that was a good idea. Municipal politicians jammed the phone lines to Victoria like teenagers trying to win tickets to a Michael Jackson concert in a radio call-in contest. Vander Zalm's colleagues in the cabinet and caucus got the message: the planning bill would not make the list of government initiatives for the next sitting of the legislature.

Vander Zalm threw a snit. He quit the cabinet and quit politics, calling his former colleagues gutless for not sharing his own estimation of his abilities. Then he sat out an election, waiting for an opportune moment to return to public life.

And return he did in the summer of 1986, at the head of a wave of new-right evangelical Christians who flooded into Social Credit's ranks and overturned everybody's applecarts. The party establishment never noticed until it was too late. They figured the post-Bennett leadership race would be a struggle within the inner circle. But while the old-line warhorses intrigued against each other, the Zalmoids were out selling memberships by the congregation-load. The clean and shiny fundamentalists packed the meetings that selected delegates to the leadership convention.

By the time Social Credit gathered at the Whistler ski resort, Vander Zalm had all the momentum. The turning point came on the third ballot. Bud Smith, a backroom heavy who controlled the Cariboo and the Southern Interior, correctly gauged the direction of the shifting political winds and spread his sails to accompany Vander Zalm's flotilla.

The ensuing election campaign consisted largely of Vander Zalm and his wife, Lillian, who for no known reason usually wore an athletic headband, smiling at voters and pronouncing everything to be "fantaaaastic!" The wheels fell off the NDP's wagon in their leader's opening press conference; an attack of nerves dried up Bob Skelly's throat, giving BCTV twenty seconds of embarrassing videotape that they replayed time and again until voting day.

"Fantaaaastic," said Vander Zalm on election night.

But his administration turned out to be a lot more than a lot of people had bargained for, and soon everybody except the Zalmoids and the NDP strategists wanted him removed from power. Under Willie Wooden Shoes, the Socreds lost five byelections in three years, including two in up-country seats that should have been rock solid. By late 1989 province-wide polls showed the government twenty-four points behind the opposition.

If the Socreds had to face a general election under their shovel-signing premier, the province would belong to the NDP's new leader, Mike Harcourt. A former three-term mayor of Vancouver, he was a long-range and patient thinker whose Mr. Average public persona concealed more political savvy than most of the candidates the New Democrats attracted.

The problem in removing Vander Zalm, Pastorel told us, was that the same divisions that had weakened the party establishment at Whistler were still unhealed. Of the three heavies who had wrestled with each other while Vander Zalm cornered the party, only Bud Smith was left in cabinet, holding down the attorney general's job while also serving unofficially as chief patronage dispenser. He was well positioned to make a move.

Grace McCarthy and Brian Smith had stepped away from the chaos, choosing their exit lines carefully. They had resigned from cabinet on matters of principle and now sat as ordinary MLAs on the government side of the house. Brian Smith was opting out of the contest, accepting a federal appointment from Brian Mulroney to become chairman of the Canadian National Railway.

That left Grace and Bud. Either one had the clout and the public stature to lead a revolt, but the first to make a move against the premier's chair would meet with a howling assault from Vander Zalm's outraged true believers, which would almost certainly end its target's political career.

"It's a Mexican standoff," was Pastorel's conclusion. "If Grace fires the opening shot, Bud will mop up. If Bud bites the bullet, Grace picks up all the marbles."

It amazed me how many clichés he could pack into so few words. Not for the first time I thought to myself, *What does Karen see in this guy?* And once again I avoided the obvious answer: he was a winner, and she liked winners.

"So what we need here is somebody else, somebody without an existing power base within the party, somebody who can rally support from all camps, somebody who can take over the party," he said. He looked to Karen.

"And that somebody is Tony Migliorini," she said.

She tapped the pile of papers in front of her. "You've all seen the focus group results — well, you haven't, Sid, but I'll show them to you if you want. Miggs tests unbelievably well across all the demographics that count, particularly with the young urban segment which is a key bloc. Nineteen out of twenty people can identify him without a prompt, and he does not bring out a single negative association even when we push for it. He's perfect."

"Perfect bothers me," said Gershom. "Is he maybe too good to be true?"

"Is he controllable?" Fornoy asked.

"As much as we need him to be," said Pastorel, and I thought, *You don't know Miggs as well as you think you do.*

"The main thing is," said Lloyd Mackenzie, "he's the best shot we've got." He leaned forward and ran his hand over his bald spot. "Look, the premier's troops control the party apparatus. We saw what happened when the dissidents tried to get a secret ballot on a leadership review at last year's convention in Penticton. They never had a chance.

So there is not going to be a nice way to do this. We've got four MLAs who have left the caucus and are waiting for someone to lead them. It's not going to be Grace or Bud, but it's got to be somebody and it's got to be soon, or the bubble will just deflate."

Pastorel weighed in again, managing to use "window of opportunity," "locking the stable door," and "go for the gold" in almost one breath. The money men made up their minds.

"All right," said Gershom and looked to Fornoy. "You on board, Walter?"

Fornoy laid his hands flat on the table and blew out his cheeks. "Under the terms we discussed."

Gershom looked at Pastorel. "Do it," he said.

The backers left, leaving my ex-wife's husband looking like, as he would undoubtedly have put it, the cat that ate the canary. We got down to work.

Karen said, "We'll need a media-relations strategy. Lloyd, can you take that on?"

Mackenzie nodded. "I'll draft it up and I've got a bright young woman I can second to you to do the leg work. We'll continue to pick up her salary."

"Our people can help with organizational logistics," said Bas Cowper. "We've got a province-wide structure in place if you want to do a Chamber of Commerce speaking tour."

"We just might," said Karen. "So I guess we'd better give Sid some basic points for a road speech."

And so they did. We spent the afternoon and some of the evening designing the campaign. I concentrated on my end of things: I would have to draft a travelling speech, a basic media release and backgrounder for the tour, and an op-ed article that could be supplied to local papers in which Miggs would set out the elements of his world view.

Ostensibly he would be touring the province as a motivational speaker, raising funds for his Camp Second Chance. But if he played as well as everyone expected him to, he would gradually metamorphose into a leader-in-waiting for the beleaguered Socreds. At a key point in the tour, the four dissident MLAs would announce that they wanted Miggs and only Miggs to lead them. After a suitable pause for weighty reflection, he would bashfully accede to their request, and Vander Zalm would have a public rival for his job.

We broke up during the lull between the rush hour traffic and the downtown evening surge. Mackenzie told me he would give me a call in the next couple of weeks; his CEO would be needing a speech to the Board of Trade. Cowper trundled amiably off, and Pastorel announced that he had a meeting to go to.

Karen and I were left in the corner conference room. "You want to have dinner?" she asked.

"What about the boys?"

"They're sleeping over at a friend's. The nanny will take them there, and I'll drop in and see them on the way home."

So we walked up Georgia Street to the Hotel Vancouver. The old pile of grey granite blocks looks more and more out of place among the tinted glass towers around it but inside it still has the same appeal that used to bring the nobs in from Point Grey and Shaughnessy for prime rib and big band dancing on the roof.

The Spanish Grill was on the ground floor. We sat by a window that looked out on Hornby Street. The smoked black Alaskan cod melted in my mouth, and Karen and I had a good time, considering what there had once been between us.

"Something's different," she said over coffee.

I ducked my head, then looked her in the eye. "I met someone."

"Ah," she breathed.

"Yeah. Ah."

"Will I meet her?"

"Eventually," I said. "If things go, you know … "

"Well, don't let her take advantage of your good nature. Bargain hard this time."

"Thanks for the advice," I said, and we looked out the window across Hornby Street; somebody was beating a drum on the old courthouse steps.

My conscience was niggling at me. "Look," I said, "how tied up are you in this Migliorini thing?"

She gave me one of her appreciative stares that probed several layers beneath my surface. "Why?"

"I'm just wondering whether you're sure he'll go the distance. I wouldn't want you left holding an empty sack."

"You think he won't stand up? No long-haul strength?"

I shrugged.

"Doesn't matter." She signalled the waitress for a refill.

And then I got it. Miggs's candidacy didn't have to endure at all. He was not going to be the leader of the Social Credit party. The powerbrokers had had their fill of charismatic loners; they weren't going to replace the present one with another model, no matter how well he tested across the key demographic segments.

"He's just to get the ball rolling, isn't he?" I said.

She smiled, and for a moment I saw a strong tinge of Pastorel in her eyes.

"So who's the real client?" I said. "Amazing Grace? Bud Smith?"

She laughed. "Doesn't matter," she repeated. "In fact it's none of the above. We don't have a client. We just need to break the stalemate, get a leadership campaign going. There'll be plenty of work after that."

"But if the big guns don't support Miggs, he'll get ground into hamburger."

"He looks tough enough to me," she said.

"Yeah," I said, "but once there's a real contender, you're going to drop him, aren't you? He'll be out there on his own."

"If his campaign stalls, he can throw his support behind one of the front-runners."

I took a long breath. "Wow," I said.

"Is this a problem for you?" she asked.

I thought about it. Now I wasn't sure exactly whom I was selling out. "No," I decided. "It's not a problem."

She went off to say goodnight to our children, and I got myself a hotel room upstairs. It would all be billed back eventually to Gershom and Fornoy.

At eleven the next morning, with the sun bright over the city again, I pulled up outside Pastorel's too big, too gaudy house. It was Saturday. The twins were sitting on the front step, arguing about something, but they broke off when they saw me.

"Hey guys," I said.

"Hey Dad," said Bill. He was tall, lean and blond, after Karen's family. Dick was only a little shorter but looked more earthbound because he had inherited the strong build and dark hair that run through my side of the family. Nobody believed they were twins; they looked like one of those near-in-age twosomes that couples sometimes produce when they're in too much of a hurry to space their children properly.

"Where do you want to go?"

"McDonald's," said Bill.

"Science World," said Dick.

That's what they'd been arguing about when I drove up. "How about we hit Mickie D's, then check out the bells and whistles?" I said.

"Deal," said Dick.

"Yeah, OK," said Bill.

So we loaded up on McNuggets and Quarter Pounders on West Broadway and bombed down to the old Expo site on False Creek, where the former B.C. Pavilion had metamorphosed as a science centre for kids. The building was a giant, multifaceted steel golf ball at the water's edge. Inside were a slew of hands-on science experiments that my kids loved, as well as an Omnimax theatre.

Right now the place also featured a display of half-life-size animated dinosaurs, honking and flexing their compressed air-powered muscles.

The twins pronounced the exhibit to be excellent and spent an hour poking around it. Then we went downstairs to the cafeteria for more food. I watched the two of them do brother things with each other at the table. They didn't bicker much; mostly they were good with each other. I didn't see any strain in them. They were holding up.

Bill looked over his root beer at me with that same cool,

considering gaze he used to give me from his playpen. Then he smiled.

"So how's it going?" I asked.

He swirled the ice around in the paper cup. "You mean with mom and Lyle and us?"

Smart kid, I thought.

"Yeah."

"It's OK, I guess. He tries when he's there. Mostly he's not there."

Neither was Karen, at least not often enough, I was thinking. Sure, my kids were living in a fancy house, getting a fancy private education. But what about the things they weren't getting, like parents who did more than fit them in between meetings?

Back when I'd been looking ahead to movie bucks, I'd thought about reopening the custody arrangements. Maybe I could still do that even without a lot of money. I set that notion down somewhere in the back of my mind, to let it sit there while I got used to the novel idea that I might take full charge of my life again. Hanging out with Mo and Miggs seemed to have side effects.

Bill slurped the last of the root beer. Dick copied him, then topped his performance with a stentorian belch.

"Can we come and stay with you when school's out?" Dick said. "Like for a couple of weeks?"

"Yeah, I want you to. I think we should spend more time together."

"Good." They smiled at each other.

In the evening we went to an early movie — *Star Trek IV*, the only funny one they made — then ate pizza. I delivered them, tired and happy, to their mother in time for bed. An hour later I was on the last sailing out of Horseshoe Bay bound for Nanaimo and the long drive home.

I went out on the ferry's upper deck. The moon was dribbling a string of silver across the choppy waters of the Strait, and the wind was cold. I tucked my hands into my pockets and let the rushing air chill my face. I thought about the kids, about Karen, about Mo.

Maybe it was just the dramatic setting, but I had the feeling that I had come, suddenly and unexpectedly, to one of life's cusps. Things were going to change. I was going to change.

I'd spent the better part of a decade with my nose pointed at the ground, dealing with nothing more than right now and whatever was right in front of me. No plans, no direction, no centre to the world, like that guy in the old Ian and Sylvia song: "You ain't livin' boy. You're just gettin' up each day and walkin' around."

I leaned into the wind that flushed the ferry deck, sucked its cold edge into my lungs and watched the vast bulk of Bowen Island slip by on the starboard side. Now, for the first time in a long time, it looked as if I had a couple of landmarks to navigate by. Between Mo and the twins, I might somehow lay out a course and go somewhere.

I didn't know where the somewhere would be, but at least I was interested in finding out.

It was well past midnight when I pulled into my driveway. I didn't remember leaving a light on in the kitchen. I went around the back of the house, climbed the stairs to the sundeck and edged up to the window in the back door.

The little white curtains left by the previous owner were filmy enough to see through into the lighted room. A man was sitting at my kitchen table, drinking steaming coffee from one of my mugs. Beside his chair was a square, hefty briefcase, the kind lawyers carry.

But the man at the table was not a lawyer. He was Leonard Geisel.

Seven

LONG, LONG AGO, HER Majesty's Royal Navy fearlessly cleansed the seven seas of ruthless pirates, driving many of them to seek new careers as promoters on the Vancouver Stock Exchange.

That's historically inaccurate but a fair characterization of some of the rogues who infest North America's most infamous stock market. By its own admission the VSE is not a place where widows and orphans should hazard their scanty troves of dimes and nickels. It is, in the judgement of the prestigious *Forbes* business magazine, "the scam capital of the world."

The VSE's vice-president of public affairs, a tough-minded ex-journalist, had been an occasional client in other public-relations jobs before he took on the Sisyphean task of trying to shore up the exchange's shaky image; Hercules had an easier time with Augeas's dung-choked stables. From time to time he'd hired me to do small pieces for the VSE newsletter, and I'd picked up a rough understanding of what made Vancouver's small exchange different from the more staid institutions in Toronto or New York.

The TSE and NYSE were where the blue-chip companies were listed, big corporations like Canadian Pacific and the Royal Bank, which had tangible assets that made money, out of which they paid their shareholders quarterly dividends. Depending on how well the company did, its stock rose or fell. Most of the companies listed on the VSE had no assets other than the hopes and dreams of the people who incorporated them, and a few stocks had nothing behind them but a ring of slick operators who artificially inflated the share price until it was time to make a killing.

Vancouver specialized in venture capital issues. Venture capital was high-risk money for fledgling resource or technology companies, trading at a few pennies a share, that came to the market looking for funds to explore for gold on a stretch of northern moose pasture or to develop some untried piece of hardware.

Most of these high-risk ventures were straight up and on the level, although the odds against their achieving their corporate goals were not demonstrably better than those printed on the back of a lottery ticket. But every now and then, underneath the stretch of moose pasture that a VSE-listed company needed funds to explore, there was an actual vein of gold.

Legitimate fortunes had been made on the VSE. Lucky "mom and pop" investors had bought stock in the exchange's listings at thirty cents a share and sold out for seventy dollars. Canada's biggest gold mine — the Hemlo deposit north of Lake Superior — had been capitalized through Vancouver. So had the country's only diamond mine, dug out of the tundra around Yellowknife, to the amazement of the South African-based cartel that controls the world market in sparkling crystallized carbon and keeps the price unnaturally high.

But overshadowing the above-board bonanzas were the institutionalized frauds that went after investors' savings like a vacuum cleaner hunting dust bunnies. Some of the scams were blatant enough to have become legendary — like the worthless company fronted by Saudi arms-dealer and Iran-Contra player Adnan Khashoggi, which flat out claimed to have found King Solomon's mines somewhere in Africa.

Then there was Med-Tech Systems Inc., which jumped onto the AIDS bandwagon just as the first panic began rolling through North American culture. Med-Tech offered a spray-on virus killer for toilet seats and telephones. The stuff was nothing more than liquid bleach.

There was Current Technologies Corp., which marketed an electrified, cone-shaped metal hat that was supposed to cure baldness.

But the basic stock-in-trade of the VSE scammer was

the technique of false underwriting. It would usually begin with a gaggle of corrupt operators breathing life into a failed junior mining-exploration company by taking over its defunct listing on the exchange. They would issue low-priced stock or "warrants" which could be converted into shares at a later date.

These preliminary issues would be by "private placements," insider deals that made sure control of the shell company ended up in the hands of friends and family. On the VSE, the ring of traders who bought cheap shares in these soon-to-be-inflated companies were called "bottom feeders."

The bottom feeders would trade shares back and forth to each other, each crooked trader operating behind a phalanx of phony accounts. The constantly increasing activity in the company's stock made the listing look hot and drove up the price. In the meantime some dodgy stockbrokers would be let in for a taste of the sugar. For a little under-the-table juice, they would begin touting the stock to their clients, whose subsequent purchases of small blocks of stock would further heat up the listing.

The shell company's directors would cloud investors' minds further by issuing puffed-up press releases that hinted at unverifiable assay results based on test cores from an exploratory drilling program that had probably never taken place.

Rumours would fly. Tips would pass from tout to tout. Everybody would be talking up the hot new listing. The ever-hopeful punters would be crowding the phones to their brokers, trying to get in before the boat sailed, buying, buying, buying. The listing's quoted price would go from eighty cents to a dollar-ten to one-sixty-five in a morning, and as the precipitous rise lured throngs of latecomers, the stock's value would soar.

That's when the bottom feeders, who had bought hundreds of thousands of shares at ten or fifteen cents each, would begin "blowing off" their holdings. They would feed their shares into the buying frenzy, a few thousand at a time, at prices that won the crooks profits of five and ten thousand percent.

Eventually the Securities Commission would come sailing up, cannons blazing, just about the time the pirates had cleaned out the marks and hauled their loot over the horizon. A press release clarifying the actual status of the venture would be ordered, and the burnt-out shell of the scam company would be abandoned and set adrift.

A year or so later the main players would resurface to do it all over again, and the bottom feeders would reform their shoals. And chances were, one of the small fry snapping at the financial morsels dripping from the mouths of the bigger fish would be the man sitting in my kitchen, drinking my coffee.

Geisel turned as I came through the kitchen door. "Hey, howya doin'?" he said.

I went right to the front of the house and peeked through the living-room curtains, half expecting to see Lou Savelek happily skipping up the walk, slipping into his brass knuckles and looking forward to a solid night's work. But there was nothing out there except one of Vancouver Island's diminutive deer munching my neighbour's shrubbery, not an uncommon sight in Comox.

I came back into the kitchen. "How'd you get in here?" I asked.

"The back door was open."

"No it wasn't."

"Well, OK, technically it wasn't open. But it only took like ten seconds with a credit card. You should think about getting some real locks, even out here in the boonies." He sipped his coffee. "You can't be too careful."

"Obviously. Now what the hell are you doing in my kitchen?"

He leaned back in the chair. "I'm visiting you. It's a thing people do."

He was giving me his Mr. Trust Me face. Any widows and orphans seeing that face had better glom on tight to their piggy banks. I said, "No sale, man. It's a thing friends do, and we're not friends."

He segued over to Mr. Aw Shucks. "Jeez, Raff, I figured

what the hell, I was spending a couple days on the island, I'd drop in, you know … "

"Just cut to Story B, would you, Weasel? This is no friendly visit. I've already had two inquiries about you."

That stopped him. "Whattaya mean? Somebody been asking about me?" There was no artifice in his face now. He just looked scared.

"Yeah. A little old man in the back room of a laundry plant. Sent a guy called Lou Savelek and another one might have been a clean-shaven sasquatch over to bring me in."

Something cold must have walked up Geisel's spine; he shook like a wet dog. "What did they want to know?"

"They wanted to know where you were. I got the impression the information had some significance to them."

The Weasel's hand shook so badly, some coffee spilled onto his wrist. The cup rattled as he set it down. "This is not funny, Raff."

"Oddly enough, that was precisely my feeling when they stuffed me into a sleeping bag and put me in the trunk of their car."

"Oh, shit. You tell 'em anything?"

"I couldn't. I didn't know anything. I'm just glad they decided to ask nicely." I took out my wallet, found the slip of paper and handed it to him. "Here, they said I should call this number. They gave me two grand. You better call them."

The Weasel placed the slip of paper on the table and stared at it. "Jesus," he said.

"Then there's door number two," I said and told him that behind that one was a cop called Conroy from the Coordinated Law Enforcement Unit. "He also wants a word."

"CLEU?" Geisel said. He laid his arms on the table and let his head drop onto them. "I'm dead," he said.

I said nothing.

After a minute he looked up. "No I'm not," he said. "You gotta help me, Raff."

"I don't think so."

"You gotta. Listen, I've done some stuff, made some deals. There's big money, really big money, in this."

"Then you can afford a really big funeral."

"Shit. Lemme think."

I let him. While he sat there and stared at the table top, I boiled the kettle and made a pot of tea. In my house, coffee is only for those who don't know any better.

I poured a cup and sat down across from him. I could almost hear the gears turning in his head.

"Listen," he said, "There's got to be a way out of this. Before, I was thinking I just needed to come over here, keep out of the mix for a few days, things'd settle down. Now, I dunno. I'm hotter than I thought."

"What did you do, Weasel? Did you steal money from the mob?"

He gave me Mr. Wide Eyes. "No way. Well, not exactly.
I kinda borrowed a hundred gees, coupla days, made a little side deal on a stock I heard about. I was gonna pull the
money out of the side deal, put it back into the client's
account. But then, wham, the Commission steps in, drops
a deep freeze on the deal."

I understood about a tenth of that. But in the next few
minutes I managed to draw the whole story out of the
Weasel. It wasn't hard; he was actually proud of what he'd
pulled off. He'd been wanting to tell somebody all about it.

There was a brokerage house — one of the big ones —
that did business with some of the more prominent criminal organizations on the west coast. The loosey-goosey
VSE was an ideal place for laundering mob money because
it was a place where illicit funds could be diverted into
legitimate or semi-legitimate investments.

To fuzzify their activities, the big brokerage houses
pieced out some of the mob business to little operations
like Geisel, Chelmsford. It was a spider's web of a dozen or
so hole-and-corner brokers, and around that web stocks
and warrants could be bought and sold. Money came in
reeking of casino skims, hookers' tricks and street-corner
dope deals, and emerged as sweet-smelling corporate capital — money invested in legitimate companies. And corporate capital was not considered income, so it was tax free
to boot.

The Weasel made a standard but steady commission out of being one of the spiders who shifted the mob's money around. But then he was offered an opportunity to bottom-feed on a false underwriting being set up by a promoter he had done deals with before. A ring of VSE operators were setting up to give a little junior mining company, White Heart Resources, the full treatment. A patch of Kootenay mountainside on which White Heart had exploration rights was about to be hyped as a potential Hemlo-sized gold deposit. It was a complete scam from front to back, but the people behind it were experienced at fleecing the lambs who bought stocks at the VSE. Geisel had been let into the fringes of the ring's operations before.

Now they were asking him if he wanted to move up into the middle of the food chain. Instead of crumbs and morsels, this time he could take a big bite. He stood to make a virtually risk-free three thousand percent profit — thirty dollars for every buck he put in — but there was one hitch. The minimum buy-in was twenty thousand dollars, and the Weasel was experiencing a bubble in his cash flow. It was too good a score to pass up, but there was nowhere he could borrow twenty grand fast without having to tell the lender about the scam. In which case, the few people who might have considered fronting him that kind of money would have wanted at least half the proceeds —

that's if they hadn't just stepped over him and taken the opportunity for themselves.

So, desperate to get in on his first big score, the Weasel dipped into the only source of serious ready money he had access to: he borrowed from one of the spider web of mob accounts, a shell company that converted skim money into stocks, held them for a week or two, then sold them on to the next stage of the laundry process.

Buying into the phony stock scam was illegal. Using the mob's money to do it was dumb. But it was typical of Leonard Geisel that, once he let greed get a choke hold on self-preservation, he would set new standards for stupidity: instead of borrowing the twenty thousand he needed, he took a hundred grand from the kind of people who wouldn't mind killing him for a nickel.

"Nobody checks these accounts, day to day," he told me. "I mean, OK, the money's not there when the time comes to move it along, then there's trouble. But I figured I'd have converted the warrants, blown off the stock and put the hundred large back where it came from before anybody knew it wasn't there."

"So what happened?"

"So the Securities Commission suddenly springs a surprise. They put a trading freeze on a coupla dozen companies they think maybe smell a little hinky. And one of them's the company I borrowed the hundred from."

A trading freeze was just like what Revenue Canada had done to my bank accounts one difficult year. Nobody could buy or sell so much as a penny's worth of the company's stock until officialdom ordained a thaw.

"So you can't put the money back," I said.

"No. Not until they lift the freeze. That could be any day. All I gotta do is stay out of sight until that happens."

I thought about it for a moment. "Let me get this straight. Nobody knows that hundred thousand is missing except you, right?"

"Right."

"So why do so many people want to talk to you?"

He looked at his hands. "That's the part that bothers me too. It's gotta be because of the freeze."

"Has it got anything to do with High Country Mining?" I asked.

"What? Nah, separate deal. By the way, you owe me for the money I fronted you on that brochure, now it's dead."

"Well, why don't I pay you out of the reward your mob buddies will give me for turning you over to them?"

His face froze, then cracked as he tried to force a smile. "Hah hah," he said. "You can forget that grand you owe me. Listen, I'll make a new deal with you. You help me get out from under this, I'll pay you … "

I could see fear wrestling with calculating greed. "Ten grand," he said.

Common sense said, *Throw this guy out now.* Whatever he was into, I'd be out of my depth. But if I'd ever had any common sense I wouldn't have grown up to be a free-lancer. I'd now spent ten years of my life in the do-a-job-get-a-cheque maze, wandering around looking for the exit.

I'd thought the movie deal was my way out and I remembered how it had felt to be winning, at least until Erlenmeyer's heart attack slammed the door on my toe just as I went to step through. Now here was the Weasel sitting at my kitchen table, and maybe those were the words "this way out" glowing in neon letters over his head.

"Fifty," I said.

"Shit on you! Twenty."

"Fifty. On fifty I can sit back for two years and try being a real writer. Two years of that is enough to make me risk what I'm going to risk, helping you. And you can afford it. How much you clear on that stock? Millions, right?"

He made that noise he always made when people wanted his money. I didn't care.

"This is a situation where people can get killed," I said. "People being me. Fifty is cheap."

"Thirty-five," he tried.

"Fifty is the price. And the deal is about to be taken off the table. I bet I can get twenty just calling that number."

His hand convulsively clutched at the piece of paper, and he made that noise again. Then he swallowed. "Fifty," he said.

"We'll make it official," I said and took him into the office. Five minutes later the laser printer rolled out a promissory note, and Geisel signed it. I folded the paper and put it in my wallet.

"Now," I said. "What do you want me to do?"

"Well, see, I was gonna ask you to put me up a coupla days."

"I don't think that's too smart. People have been coming here looking for you. The cops are keeping tabs on your cellular. Every time you tried to call me, they turned on their tape recorders."

The lights came on in the Weasel's head. "Shit!" he said. "The friggin' phone? The cops been listening in? Oh, shit and shit again! No wonder they're looking for me." He stared straight ahead for a long beat. "Now this begins to make some sense," he said.

"Tell me how," I said.

"Computer guy told me they could do this now. I thought he was blowing smoke, you know? But the cops, they set up a scanner, hook it up to a big computer, then they listen in on all the cellular frequencies. They got the computer set to kick in anytime it hears a particular word."

He got up, went to the counter and poured another cup of coffee. "Like, say they're interested in So-and-so Resources Company. Well, every time anybody says that name, right, the computer records what the guy says and notes down what his cellular frequency is. Then they can just listen in on that frequency all the time."

I got it. I said, "They were scanning for any mention of those dodgy companies the Commission is sniffing at. They catch you saying the secret word, so they begin collecting all your hits. Then, bang, you disappear, the little old man in East Vancouver starts asking around after you, so then the cops get really interested."

"Yeah." I could see he was putting it together in his head. "Look, Raff," he said, "I can be pretty dumb sometimes but I ain't totally gonzo. I know cellulars aren't secure. I never said anything on the phone that could hurt me or my associates in court."

"So?"

"So the cops have nothing on me. All I need is to talk to the guys in Vancouver, let them see there's no problem, the money's not missing or anything, and I'm cool."

"What about the cops?"

"If I can lose the heat from my clients, then there's no hook for Conroy to put in me. I sit still, say nothing, and I'm OK."

"So, again, what do you want me to do?"

He lifted the briefcase from beside his chair and put it on the table. "Hold this for me," he said.

"What is it?" I asked.

"A little over three million dollars," he said.

The briefcase was big but not that big, I thought. Then he showed me. The case was filled with bearer bonds in denominations of five thousand and ten thousand dollars. When he'd unloaded his blocks of worthless stock, he'd taken payment in negotiable securities, which were as good as cash at any bank in the world.

"You're going to trust me with three million dollars in bearer bonds?" I asked. "What makes you think I won't run away with it?"

"Well, you might run away with three million of my money. But this will only stay mine as long as nobody but us knows about it. You screw off with it, I'm going to tell that old man you talked to that it's his money, and you've got it. How long you think it would take him to find you?"

I'd seen *Charlie Varrick* and all the other movies about people who steal from the guys with bent noses. "Deal," I said.

We stashed the briefcase in a cupboard under the kitchen sink.

"Now, first thing in the morning," the Weasel said. "I got to get a phone I can rely on. Where would you go in this town to buy things that fall off the back of a truck?"

There was a second-hand store I had been into, with an owner who looked like he might have trouble providing a bill of sale for every item in stock.

"I'll start there," the Weasel said. "If I come up dry, is there a bar where bikers hang out?"

I told him I'd seen Harley-Davidsons outside the Courtenay Hotel beer parlour.

"That'll do," he said. "Where can I sleep?"

I laid the couch cushions on the floor of the spare bedroom. I had planned to buy bunk beds for when the twins visited but I hadn't got around to it yet. "For fifty grand, I should get your bed," Geisel said.

"I'll let you have it for another ten," I said.

He declined the transaction, and I went to bed. I fell asleep fast but awoke suddenly in the cold hour before dawn in a full-blown anxiety attack. I hadn't had one of those nocturnal chillers since the bad days of the big recession, when I'd lost my job, my kids and most of my self-respect.

I fought down the panic, but even when the symptoms had dwindled, I had to admit that I was risking a lot by tying my fate to that of a notorious scam artist — certainly my health and maybe even my life. Lying there in sweaty sheets, with the last of the moonlight creeping up the bedroom wall, I felt like a lost and abandoned child.

But I remembered what Mo Migliorini had said: "Sometimes you fish, sometimes you cut bait. Make up your mind!" And I remembered Miggs's all-purpose "Don't stop trying."

Tough it out, I told myself. *The rainbow may be shit, but the gold at the end is real.*

I fell back asleep just as the sun was coming up and woke up again in the middle of the morning. The Weasel was gone, and so was my car, but the briefcase was still where we'd hidden it.

I felt pretty thinned out, but breakfast and a pot of tea worked as a partial restorative. I read the city dailies in my sun-drenched kitchen. The previous owner's taste ran to gold and white, so the room reminded me of my plate of fried eggs, but the brightness was some help against depression.

Things were getting kind of crazy in Eastern Europe, the front pages said. *Suppose they gave a dictatorship of the proletariat and nobody came,* I thought. The cold war was melting into the corners of history, and George Bush was saying something about a new world order. It sounded to me as if he needed a new speechwriter.

Over on the provincial news pages, everybody was hammering away at Bill Vander Zalm. The four dissident MLAs were still out of the government caucus, the premier's leadership rivals were still keeping their heads down and the media were still combing the province trying to find Social Credit constituency association executives who could be coaxed into saying uncomplimentary things about their boss. They were having some success.

I cleaned up after myself, then went into the office and started work on the Miggs material. I had a bundle of notes

and jottings from the meeting at Pastorel's and I began
putting together a release and a backgrounder that expressed
the themes we had decided on.

I worked until early afternoon, then took a break for
lunch. I was heating my soup when the back door opened
and Geisel slid into the room. In his hand was a cellular
phone.

"Got one," he said. "Cost me a hundred but it's fresh
and good for at least a month."

This time I knew what he was talking about. I'd once
written a speech for a phone company executive about
communications security. So I knew that the cellular phone
the Weasel held was a clone of a legitimate instrument
owned by some unsuspecting subscriber. The clone phone's
ID chip had been reprogrammed to operate on the same
frequency as the straight unit. As far as the cellular company
was concerned, a call generated on the Weasel's new phone
was coming from its subscriber's instrument, and the charges
would appear on his account. At the end of the month,
when the bill arrived, the subscriber would go stratos-
pheric, and the fraud would be discovered. In the meantime Geisel had unlimited and untraceable phone service.

"OK," he said, "let's get busy." He dialled a number.
"There's this guy I know, he's connected. I'll call him, feel
it out." He waited while the phone rang. I watched him
put on his Mr. Hi-How-Are-Ya face.

"Hey," he said, "that you, Albie? Yeah, Lennie Geisel, how's it goin'?" He listened. "Nah, I been outta town. Tell you the truth, I been shacked up with this lady, got a cabin in the Gulf Islands, been doing a little deep-sea diving, you know what I mean." He listened again. "Whattaya tellin me, Albie? I don't know nothin' about this. I been pissed drunk mosta the past week." Listening. "No shit? Well, listen, you call 'em, tell 'em you heard from me, I'm on my way to see 'em right now." Listening. "Nah, I got no problems. Everything's straight, totally copacetic. Yeah, talk to ya."

He hung up, crossed his fingers. "Now the hard part," he said. "Take me down to Nanaimo, I'll walk on the ferry, bus it into town."

I took him down the highway, an hour and a half to Nanaimo. He kept twisting around in his seat, as if he couldn't get comfortable. "Why you drive this piece of crap?" he asked.

"It builds character."

The Weasel looked out the window, scraped his lower teeth over his upper lip. "Gotta work," he told himself, then said nothing more until I dropped him off at the ferry terminal.

I drove back home in the deepening twilight, heated up a canned steak and kidney pie for supper and watched the news. I thought about doing some more work on the Miggs stuff but I was too bagged after a bad night.

Instead, I watched Teri Garr light up the Letterman show which aired in Comox at nine-thirty, courtesy of the Detroit NBC station WDIV. The local cable plucked the American station's satellite signal and delivered it to us three hours ahead of KING-TV out of Seattle.

At ten-thirty, Letterman said go to bed and I took his advice. I turned in hoping to dream about Teri Garr but instead I slept solidly and got up early. By eight forty-five, I was showered and shaved, full of toast and tea, and ready to hack out Miggs's road speech. I powered up the computer and loaded the out-of-date WordStar word processing program. Most writers had switched to MS Word or WordPerfect, but I had invested a lot of time learning all the two-key codes for WordStar and I hated to see the effort go to waste.

People have sometimes asked me how I go about writing speeches. If I feel the need to astound them with my capacities as a wordsmith, I give them a plausible spiel about how I analyse the speaker's intent and the audience's interests, then subtly craft imagery and trigger words into a composite whole that will put across the right impression.

If I feel honest, I tell them that I don't really know how I do it. I might sketch a short outline, or make a couple of notes. But mostly I turn on the computer and stare at the screen until it suddenly becomes obvious what the client should say. When that happens, it means that the little guy who lives in the back of my head has turned up for work. I write down whatever he tells me, and the result is usually a speech that does what the client needs to do.

Now I typed "Draft Road Speech, Tony Migliorini," dropped the cursor down a couple of spaces and stared at the illuminated white rectangle.

After a minute, I typed "My fellow British Columbians," then backspaced it out and put in "My friends." Then I sat and stared some more, waiting for the little guy to kick in.

Suddenly he was there. My fingers went to the keyboard. "One day a few years ago," I wrote, "I was lying on my back in a hospital bed, staring at the ceiling and wondering what life was all about."

I waited for the answer to that rhetorical question. Then it came. "It was not something I had given much thought to before," I wrote, "but when somebody suddenly takes your legs away, there isn't a whole lot you can do except try to understand why."

I backed up the cursor and turned "try to understand" into "try and understand," since the odds were ten to one that's how Miggs would say it. Speechwriting and good grammar sometimes have only the most tenuous relationship. Except on occasions of truly high-and-mighty ceremony, it's best to phrase a text in the vernacular.

Another sentence began unrolling in my head. "It occurred to me, lying in that rehabilitation ward," I wrote, "that hard times are easier to take if you believe that life has some meaning." I waited, then it came again: "Up until my accident, I had been too busy to think about what life might mean to me. Life had just been my work, my family, my friends, my fun."

I waited some more, then out it came: "After I ended up in one of these," I could see him slapping the wheel-chair arm, "I realized that I was going to have to be a little more serious, a little more thoughtful about what I would do with my life." I waited. "And that's why I'm here today."

After that, the speech wrote itself. The theme was Miggs's own slogan: "Never stop trying." It was a straight-up motivational speech but built out of images that came from Miggs's own experience: his award-winning athletic career in high school, the perils of firefighting, the hazards and triumphs of search-and-rescue patrols — then the shock of being paralysed, the resolve to rise above the disabling injury, the campaign to develop his rehab camp.

On the surface it was a fund-raising pitch to business audiences, asking them to support his Sechelt project. But the undercurrents were pure personal profile-building, positioning Miggs as the kind of public persona a lot of British Columbians — particularly those on the centre-right of the political spectrum — would find compelling.

The plan was for Tony Migliorini to tour the province in a chartered bus with his name on the side, while advance men put a full court press on local and regional media to gain coverage. We would make him flavour of the month, and his rising appeal would flow perfectly naturally into a suggestion — which would come at the right time from some well-rehearsed grassroots Socred source — that here at last was what the party was looking for.

Miggs would decline gracefully — aw shucks, I'm no politician, folks — but would continue touring and speaking. The media would be quietly advised that powerful people were taking Miggs's potential seriously. Canned letters to the editor — some of them ghosted by me — would begin to filter in to local papers.

Next there would be a press conference, where Miggs would indicate that the continual calls for him to enter politics were beginning to make him reconsider. A day or two later some retired Socred cabinet minister from the W.A.C. Bennett years, a respectable old warhorse, would personally sell Miggs a party membership. Scarcely before the ink on the card was dry, the four dissident Socred MLAs would hold their own press conference and call on Miggs to help them reform the party.

And then all hell would break loose.

I wondered how long Miggs would ride the accelerating merry-go-round before jumping clear. I doubted that he would stay long enough to be pushed off by the people Lyle Pastorel was fronting for.

I had been avoiding looking at where I stood in this burgeoning matrix of conflicting aims and convenient deceit. I wished Miggs well but I didn't really wish harm to Pastorel. And I didn't feel that I owed either of them anything more than the services I was being paid to perform.

But what about Karen and Maureen Migliorini? If it came to a clash of interests between the mother of my children and the first woman in years who had made me feel like a whole human being again, where would my loyalties lie?

The phone rang. It was Geisel in Vancouver. He'd talked on the phone to the laundry man and was going to see him at noon the next day. He would keep in touch.

"Good luck," I told him.

"The stuff is still where we left it?"

"It is."

"OK. Talk to ya." He hung up.

I noodled around with Miggs's speech until I was satisfied with it, then faxed it over to Karen. Now it was late afternoon, there wasn't much food in the fridge, and what there was had little appeal. A restaurant meal sounded like an appropriate way to celebrate doing a good job and getting well paid for it.

I drove over to the Old House in Courtenay, had a prime rib steak with all the options and rolled home by eight o'clock.

There was a well-used Hyundai sedan in my driveway. I recognized it at once. I parked on the street and got out. Maureen Migliorini came around the side of the house.

"I was in the backyard, thinking about your garden," she said.

"What garden?" I said.

"That's what I was thinking."

We stood on the front lawn, a few metres apart. "The last ferry back to Sechelt sailed an hour ago," she said. "You'd better invite me in."

"Come in," I said.

Eight

"I WAS READING IN *Cosmo* or *Chatelaine* or somewhere that you can tell a lot about a man by the state of his garden," she said. It came out a little too fast. She was nervous. So was I.

"I don't have a garden," I said. That was true. There were some trees, there was some lawn, and there could have been a flower bed under the weeds beside the garage, but if that constituted a garden, it was entirely by default. I asked, "Does that make me a man of mystery?"

She sighed. "You'd better not be. I've had enough of that."

We were sitting in the living room; she'd taken the middle of the couch and I had taken the armchair. The kettle was on in the kitchen.

"Do you want to tell me about that?" I said. It sounded like the right kind of thing to say. It beat "What the hell are you doing here?"

"There was a man I was seeing in Vancouver after the divorce. He worked for a client." She paused. "I haven't even told you what I do for a living, have I?" She patted her thigh, said, "Well done, Mo." She shook her head. "I organize offices for people. I come in and tell them who should be let go and who should stay, and which jobs should be combined or shrunk or expanded. I used to do it for a management consulting firm. Now I am a management consulting firm."

"I'm impressed," I said. I was.

"Anyway," she said, "there was this man and we hit it off — lunch, then dinner, then a weekend out at Harrison Lake. It was the first time since the divorce, he made me feel good and I was thinking, *This could work long-term, maybe,* and then I saw him at the Granville Island market with his wife and his kids, and … you know how it is."

I didn't, really, but I could imagine. "I'm sorry," I said.

"So … " She put her hands together in her lap and looked at them. "So, this time I thought I'd just cancel out any possibility of surprises. I came over here to find out if maybe you had a wife or kid, before anything" — she opened her hands — "else happened. It made sense this morning. Now I feel more than a little dumb."

Somewhere along the way, I'd learned never to tell a woman how she ought or ought not to feel. Men generally don't mind being told how to react to emotional situations; most of us have only the sketchiest notion of where our feelings might be at any particular time and we are grateful for occasional directions. But not women: they don't like it.

The kettle started to squeak next door. I got up to go make the tea. She didn't follow me into the kitchen. When I came back with cups and necessities on a tray, she was looking at an old photo of Karen and the twins on the mantelpiece.

"You won't find us all together at the market," I said.

She turned and faced me. "I'm treating you pretty badly."

I put the tray down on the coffee table. "No," I said. "You probably have no idea how much good you're doing me."

"I guess we should talk."

"I think we're about to."

And we did, for the next several hours. It was like one of those college-age gab sessions that range from airy speculation about the purpose of life to giggled true confessions of our most embarrassing moments. I couldn't help contrasting how it felt with the way it had been at first between Karen and me. The moment I met Karen it was as if I'd known her for years; sitting with Mo, both of us on the couch now, it was definitely two strangers getting to know each other. But the more we revealed, the more comfortable we felt. The fit was right.

By three in the morning, we were groggy and all worded out. It seemed silly for one of us to stay on the couch, so we curled together in bed and just slept. In the morning we kept getting in each other's way between the bedroom and the bathroom, until we ended up doing adolescent things with each other in the shower. Then, still wet and slippery, we did some more serious stuff on the bed and eventually slid onto the bedroom floor. She laughed afterwards, and I joined in.

Breakfast was a joint accomplishment. She complimented me on the quality of my scrambled eggs. "They're free range," I said. "One of the advantages of leaving the city."

"Downshifter," she said.

"That's me. I'm a downshifter. What are you?"

She gathered up plates and cups, took them to the sink, ran water on them. "I don't know. Maybe I'm a downshifter in the making. Or maybe it's not the small-town life that attracts me. Maybe it's just a particular small-town resident."

I followed her and put my arms around her waist, clasped them gently over her flat stomach. "I've heard about people with long-distance relationships."

"Yeah, me too," she said. "What do you say, we just keep playing it by ear?"

"They're nice ears," I said and kissed the nearest one.

"Show me your small town," she said.

ॐ

It was another of those beautiful days that Vancouver
Islanders are not supposed to tell easterners about: the sun
bright, the breezes soft, the gulls skimming the waves in
the harbour. The Rotary Club had almost finished building a boardwalk out over the rip-rap breakwater. We
walked out on the rough timbers and looked down on the
fishing boats tied up in the sheltered marina.

I drove her around to the valley's sites: the rocky beach
at Point Holmes, the sandy one at Kye Bay, the air base
where we saw a Buffalo fixed-wing rescue plane practising
search patterns. The big yellow aircraft flew out over the
sea and came back again, so incredibly slowly it seemed it
must stall and drop at any moment.

"Free air show," Mo said.

"You should be here in April," I told her. That was when
the Canadian Air Force's Snowbird aeronautics team came
to Comox for a week's practice. You could tell the old-time
valley residents from the newcomers by whether they bothered to look up when the nine red-and-white jets buzzed
the town and spun into a spiralling climb.

"Maybe I'll be here for that," she said.

We had lunch at my favourite Comox hangout, the Black
Fin Pub. It was a comfortable modern place overlooking the
marina. Whoever designed the menu had a real thing about

melted cheese, but the food was good, and the Vancouver Island-brewed Shaftebury cream ale was perfection.

"Try the perogies," I advised. She did and liked them.

We opted for the cheesecake and coffee, and I was stirring my cup when a blunt finger poked hard into my shoulder. I smelled Blue Stratos.

"Hey, wordman," said Savelek, "you seen that guy yet?"

I put down the spoon and turned in my seat. He liked it that I had to look up to him, but I wasn't going to try standing when he was crowding me.

"No," I said, "I haven't seen him."

He gave me his practised sleepy-eyed look, then slid his eyes across to Mo and ran them deliberately over her body and came back to me.

"You'll let us know if you see him."

"I'll let you know." I looked out the window.

The smell of cologne faded, which told me he was walking away.

"Was that for real?" asked Mo.

"He thinks so," I said.

"I always thought Rocky Balboa was a fictional character."

"Let's forget it."

She shrugged. "OK. Forget what?"

"Come on, I'll show you beautiful downtown Courtenay." I got up.

She rose and took my arm. "Actually, I'd like to revisit a place we've already seen."

"Sure. Where?"

She ran her fingertips up the inside of my arm. I shivered. "Your place," she whispered.

"You're on."

The Black Fin is built on a slope, with a small parking lot. Just up the hill is a vacant lot for overflow parking during peak hours. I had parked in the lower area, near the front door. Now, as I nosed the Concord down the short driveway to the street, I heard an engine starting in the upper lot. I swung uphill onto Port Augusta Street and looked right. A brown and tan Volkswagen bus was exiting the overflow lot onto the side street that ran into Port Augusta. I recognized the driver.

"Look," I said. "It's our friend with the video camera."

Mo turned to track him as we drove past the side street. "He's following us."

I tapped the steering wheel and made up my mind. "The hell with him. We'll go back to my place; if he hangs around outside, I'll call the cops and have him busted for being a peeping tom."

I continued up to the intersection of Port Augusta and Comox Avenue, the town's main drag, and turned left. Seconds later my rearview mirror showed Gilfillan's VW edging around the corner and following us. He remained a discreet distance behind all the way back to my house.

I put the Concord in the driveway with its motor still running and looked back over the front seat to see what the private detective would do. The bus stopped at the curb a few doors up the street, engine idling. Gilfillan made no move to get out.

I killed the Concord's engine. Gilfillan shut down the VW.

"Now what?" I wondered.

"Get outta the car," said a voice in my left ear. I turned to see the barrels of a sawed-off shotgun centimetres from my face. I very carefully opened the door.

The gun was wrapped in brown paper, with only the ends of the twin barrels showing. It was in the oil-stained hands of a skinny, acne-scarred man in his twenties. He wore black jeans and a T-shirt that had "AC/DC" printed on it in gothic lettering, and he smelled like nervous sweat. He gestured toward the house. "Inside," he said. "Now."

Another young man, this one paunchy and hairy, got out of a beat-up red pickup truck parked on the street. His right hand was wrapped around something bulky in the pocket of his khaki jacket. He walked up to the Concord's passenger door, opened it and motioned Mo to follow me. We all went into the house.

The big one closed the door behind us. Skinny said,

"On the couch," to Mo and me, and "Check it out," to Paunchy. Mo and I sat down, with the shotgun levelled at us. The big guy took a stubby black handgun out of his jacket and went to check the other rooms. It didn't take long. He was back in a minute. "All clear," he said.

"Give me your wallet," said Skinny. I took it out of my hip pocket and handed it over. He dug out my driver's licence and I could see him comparing my face to the picture. He tossed it back to me.

"OK, watch 'em," he said to the big one. Paunchy leaned against the kitchen doorway and negligently pointed the pistol at us. Skinny picked up the phone and punched in a number. I couldn't see what he dialled, but it was only seven digits. The call was local and it was answered on the first ring.

"We're in the house," he said into the phone. "We got Rafferty and a woman was with him." He listened, then nodded. "OK."

He turned to me. "Guy on the phone says you don't screw around, nothing's gonna happen to you. You give us what we came for, we're outta here, you're OK. Got it?"

I nodded. "What do you want?"

Skinny said into the phone, "What do we want?" Then to me he said, "Man says he wants what the stockbroker gave you."

"What did he give me?" I said.

Into the phone, Skinny said, "He's gettin' cute." He listened, then motioned to Paunchy.

I watched him come toward me. He tucked the pistol into the back of his jeans. When he moved, it was surprisingly swiftly and fluidly for a big man. His fist caught me on the left side of the jaw and my head snapped to the right.

I had not been punched in a long time. It hurt, first a dull ache and then a sharp stab at the hinge of my jaw, as if something had torn. My ears made noises like a truck engine revving.

Skinny said, "The stuff the stockbroker gave you."

I shook my head to clear it. "You're gonna have to be more specific," I said.

Skinny nodded to Paunchy again. I saw his right fist come up and flinched away, which put me square in the path of his left. My nose felt like a building had dropped on it. My eyes filled with water, and I felt my own blood warming my chin and dripping onto my chest.

Skinny was saying something into the phone, then he turned to Paunchy. "Smack the broad a couple times," he said.

"All right, OK. No more hero shit," I said. "Gimme something to stop this blood, I'll give you the stuff."

Paunchy went into the kitchen, came back with a tea towel. I took it and held it to my nose.

"It's under the sink," I said. "Briefcase."

The big one went back into the kitchen. I heard the noise of bottles rattling, then he returned with Geisel's case and put it on the coffee table. It was locked.

"The key," said Skinny.

If there was a key, Geisel had it. I told them that. Skinny looked like I was becoming boring. He handed the sawed-off to Paunchy, then took a butterfly knife out of his back pocket. He flicked his wrist, and the fifteen-centimetre blade snicked open. He put down the phone, took hold of the briefcase and sliced through the leather flaps above the brass locks. He kept his knife well honed.

He picked up the phone. "It's open. Whatta we lookin' for?" He listened. "OK, hold on."

He rummaged through the case. Then he turned it upside down, dumping the wads of bearer bonds onto the table, where they spilled onto the floor. He pushed them aside, scattered them around, then picked up the phone.

"There's nothin' like that here," he said. He picked up one of the bonds. "Just a lot of papers, certificates or some-thin', with 'CitiBank' on 'em." He listened again. "Yeah," he said and put the phone down.

He looked at Mo and me, held up the knife. "No more shit, asshole," he said. "You give it up now, or we cut your girlfriend's face."

Mo's voice was very, very controlled. "Raff?" she said.

I'd already said goodbye to the Weasel's three million,

including my fifty thousand. But if that's not what they were after, then I had nothing left to give them.

"Wait, wait, wait a minute," I said. "You're not here for that stuff? What the hell are you looking for?"

Skinny moved in, angling the blade so it shed light into my eyes. "I told you no more shit."

He turned toward Mo, and I shivered. It was time to do something brave and futile. But Mo beat me to it.

Maureen Migliorini sat up straight and looked Skinny in the eye. There was only the tiniest quaver in her voice as she said, "Listen, I don't know what you're looking for or who's on the end of that phone line. What I do know is there's a private detective outside with a high-resolution video camera and a directional microphone. He's got your faces and this conversation on tape, and I'd be very surprised if he hasn't also pointed that thing at your licence plate. My advice is you leave now and you leave fast."

Paunchy went to the window and looked out. Skinny said, "Don't shit me … " and then the big one came back fast.

"She's right, man," he said. "It's a big fuckin' camera, gotta dish on it, dude's aiming it right at us."

"Shit!" said Skinny. "Get out there! Get him!"

Paunchy went out the door, and Skinny grabbed the sawed-off and made to follow, then skidded to a stop in the open doorway, put the gun back on Mo and me, his head swivelling back and forth between us and what was happening outside.

I heard the VW engine rev and a squeal of tires, and from the way the skinny one tracked it, I knew that Gilfillan was putting space between him and my house.

"Fuckin' goddam!" said Skinny. He stomped the floor and yelled at his partner on the lawn. "You had a fuckin' gun, asshole! Whyncha stop him?"

I couldn't hear Paunchy's answer. But I did hear my neighbour across the street calling out, "Hey what's going on? We're calling the police!" And I thanked God for making small-town neighbours who mind each other's business.

Skinny looked as if he wanted to shoot somebody, and whether that was us, my neighbour or his buddy wouldn't have made much difference to him. "Fuck this shit!" he said, and then he was gone.

I rose up and looked out the window. Their pickup was pulling away from the curb. I knew my neighbour was straining to get the licence plate. I went out on the front step.

"It's OK," I called out. "Just a family dispute. My girl-friend's kid brother," I improvised.

The neighbour looked skeptical but he usually did. "OK," he said. "I didn't really call the cops anyway."

"Thanks. Sorry about the noise. Won't happen again."

I couldn't make out what he was saying as he went back

inside but I wouldn't have bet he was thanking God for making neighbours like me.

There was no one on the line when I picked up the phone. Mo was sitting on the couch, white and trembling. "Tell me they're gone," she said.

"You were amazing," I said.

"I was scared to death," she said. She got up and walked around, rubbing her arms as if she'd been out in a cold wind. Her knees were too loose. "What you saw there was everything I had," she said, with a shiver in her voice. "I was about ready to run for the door."

"I think we need something stronger than tea," I said.

There was a half-bottle of Jack Daniels in the kitchen. I got it and a couple of tumblers. When I came back, the briefcase was on the coffee table in front of her and Mo was putting the Weasel's bearer bonds back into it.

"There's more than two million, maybe three million dollars in negotiable securities here," she said. I didn't like the way she looked at me. "Shouldn't we be calling the police now?"

"I can't."

"That's what I was afraid of. Just what are you into, Raff?"

I poured a couple of fingers of bourbon into each glass, sat down next to her and handed her the drink. "It's a long story," I said.

She took a good swallow. "Tell it to me."

So I did. It took a while, and she spent a lot of that time staring into the air in front of her and sipping the whiskey.

"I don't like it," she said when I'd finished. "I don't like it at all. I mean, I don't know the legalities of what your friend Geisel is doing, but he clearly misappropriated a client's money and used it for his stake in what was probably a crooked deal."

When she put it that way, I had to agree with her. "So he's most likely guilty of fraud or criminal breach of trust," she went on. "And you are an accessory." She lightly punched the briefcase in front of her. "And if I pretend I never saw any of this, that makes me an accessory too."

"I'm sorry," I said.

"Me too." She stood up. "I have to go. I have to think about all of this."

She went to the door, stood there with her hand on the doorknob. I got up and went to her, put my arms around her. She leaned back against me.

"You've got to know," I said, "I've never done anything like this before. Remember when you said 'This is not me' in Sechelt? Well this is not a Sid Rafferty I'm particularly comfortable with either."

She sighed and opened the door. "I'll call you, Raff," she said. "I won't do anything before then." She kissed me on the cheek and left.

I watched her get into her old Hyundai and drive away.

Later I sat on my couch and looked at the Weasel's briefcase. I thought about an old proverb my Liverpool Irish
grandmother used to quote: "God says, 'Take what you
want, then pay.'"

Just before five o'clock Geisel called. He was driving up the
highway from Nanaimo. "It's cool," he said. "It's all cool."

"What do you mean?"

"I talked to the man. I told him I'd been out of town,
didn't know he was looking for me. We talked about that
situation, you know, like the, er, communications complications, OK? And it's all cool. They're happy, I'm happy. We
sit tight, wait for stuff to settle down, and then it's business
as usual."

I told him it had not been business as usual at my place.
I told him the basics about Skinny and Paunchy.

"I'll be there," he said. "About an hour."

It was actually less than fifty minutes. He'd moved fast.
He came in, went directly to the briefcase, looked at the
severed straps and checked the contents.

The Jack Daniels was still on the coffee table. The Weasel
took a shot straight from the bottle, wiped his mouth and
said, "What the fuck happened?"

Now I told him about the two guys with guns in full
detail, including the likelihood that my participation in the

Weasel's scheme of things had probably blown out the only chance at a relationship I'd had in years.

He wasn't interested in my emotional life. "I don't get it," he said. "Who are these guys? I mean, obviously, somebody sends them to get something, he's sitting on the end of the line telling 'em what to do. But it's not the bonds, 'cause they ignore the bonds."

"I figured it was your client from the laundry," I said.

"Yeah, but it can't be," he said. "While these guys were working you over, him and me were having our polite conversation."

We went over it several times from different angles. Somebody wanted something and they thought the Weasel had given it to me. But it wasn't the briefcase full of bonds. And we couldn't think of anything else.

"Leave it," I said. "Let's ask a different question: how did whoever it was know that you and I were in touch with each other?"

"That CLEU cop was listening in on a scanner every time I used my cellular," said Geisel.

"But we never talked on your cellular, just on the 'replacement' you organized after you got here," I said. "And Conroy said my phone wasn't tapped."

"Yeah," said the Weasel, "he said that. But did you check that out?"

I didn't know what to look for, but Geisel did. He found

it outside where the phone wire came down the side of the house after looping over from the pole. It was a black plastic box, a little smaller than a pack of cigarettes. We left it where it was and went back inside.

We went into the kitchen. Geisel turned on the radio, started up the dishwasher and ran water into the sink. "OK," he said, "let's talk."

"It's not the mob," I offered, "and it's not Gilfillan, 'cause he sure didn't hire the two bikers. Could it maybe be somebody you dealt with when you were buying that dodgy cellular?"

He thought about it. "Nah. I didn't deal with any bikers. I got the phone from the second-hand guy, he don't know me from anywhere, who I'm with."

"Then who's left?"

"The cop," he said. "Gotta be the cop."

"He didn't strike me as the bent copper type," I said.

"What are you, an experienced judge of policemen?"

I shrugged. The phone rang. I went into the living room and picked it up.

"Wordman," said the voice, "you know who this is?"

I said I did.

"We gotta talk."

"I got nothing to say to you."

"You think so?" said Savelek, and I knew he'd practised the little chuckle that came down the phone wire. "OK, so you listen. I see you today, I'm thinkin', *What if this ass-hole's shinin' me on, he hasn't seen that guy we're lookin' for. If I find this Geisel guy, that's gonna make Uncle Enzo happy.* So I wait for you to come out of the place and I take a little drive up after you and your honey.

"Then I'm down the block, I see these two losers take you in the house, then this other yo-yo has a video cam-era. Then they're runnin' around in the yard and there's some kinda shit goin' on, and they take off fast, so I think, *Let's see what the assholes in the pickup are all about,* and I fol-low them. They stop, I stop, I give them a little money, and we have a talk." He chuckled again. "You wanna know what it is we talk about?"

"Sure," I said.

"We talk about this briefcase that some stockbroker gives you, it's full of papers. These assholes, they don't know shit about this stuff. But I know. I know what you got there, wordman."

"What do you know?"

"I know you and that Weasel dipshit got something you shouldn't have. So I call my uncle, and he tells me don't worry, just a misunderstanding, it's all smoothed out. So then I know somethin' else." He paused, waiting.

"Yeah?" I said finally. "What's that?"

"I know you and the Weasel put one past the old man. That's OK with me. Way I see it, there's this buncha money goin' around loose, just waitin' for somebody to come and pick it up. I even know how much."

"You do?"

"Yeah, little over three mil."

I said nothing.

"Wordman, you want to know how I know?" I could hardly hear the last word, because Savelek's voice on the other end of the line was drowned out by the blast of a ship's whistle.

I looked at my watch; it was just past the hour. I knew that sound. It was the sound the ferry made leaving the dock at Little River just north of Comox, heading for Powell River and the Sunshine Coast.

It was the ferry Maureen Migliorini was heading for, to take her back to Camp Second Chance.

"I said, you want to know how come I know?" Savelek repeated.

There was a pause, and I heard Mo's voice say, "Raff, I'm OK. Please do as he says."

Savelek came back on the line. "Good advice, wordman. Now get me the money."

If I said, "Don't hurt her," he probably would; he was that kind. So I said, "Geisel's got it. It'll take me maybe an hour to get to him. Call me back."

There was a pause. "If you're shittin' me, you won't like it."

"I know," I said.

"No cops," he said.

"No cops." I heard him hang up.

We went back into the kitchen and turned on the noise-makers again. The Weasel was not happy. He was even less happy when I told him about Savelek. "You're not giving him my money," he said.

"I am if I have to," I said. "But I'm hoping I don't have to."

His face said forget it, but I told him, "Listen, that conversation was not private. The phone, remember? That CLEU cop would've been listening in. So, what's he gonna do?"

"We don't know what the hell's he gonna do," the Weasel bleated. "If he's crooked, he's gonna take the money and split."

"OK," I agreed. "If he's crooked, that's what he does, but I'm thinking we can set him up to deal with Savelek first. And while that's happening, we get my girl and get out of there.

"But maybe Conroy's straight, maybe the phone tap and the two guys were just a little bit of rule-bending," I continued. "Then we're still better off than trying to handle Savelek alone." I swallowed. "Cause I don't think he's gonna take money his uncle doesn't know about and then leave us walking around talking about it."

"Shit," said the Weasel.

"This is not about money anymore," I said. "It's about not dying."

He made that noise again. I wasn't listening. I was thinking. I knew how to handle Conroy.

Nine

THE CORONADO CONSTRUCTION site was brightly
lit and deserted. Not much had changed in the few days
since I had last been here, although I could see that the
cables to the gondola lift were now in place.

Geisel and I had left the car a kilometre back down the
access road at a turnaround where logging equipment was
parked for the night. We hiked up to the roadside pile of
slash and stumps banked up beside the resort's entrance
gates, then worked our way across the heaps of debris to
approach the main lodge from the rear. Geisel carried his
briefcase tight against his chest.

There were lights on in the office area where I'd met
Gaspar and Savelek: either the accountant was working late
or there was a night watchman.

I hunkered down behind an uprooted stump and
pushed the little button on my watch that lit up the display. It was just after eight. If Savelek waited the full hour

before calling back, he'd be getting my message in about ten minutes.

But Lou didn't strike me as a patient man; he had probably already called and got my answering machine, with a specially recorded announcement just for him.

"Savelek," my voice would say, "I will meet you at the Coronado resort site at nine o'clock tonight. I'll bring everything I got from Geisel."

I figured I knew what he would do the moment he got the message. And now it looked as if I'd guessed right. In the still, cold mountain air, sound travelled well. I heard a telephone ringing in the main building, the noise of the bell coming faint but clear.

The ringing stopped. I could imagine the conversation: Savelek telling whoever answered to get off the mountain now and not to come back till morning.

After a minute or so I heard the front door of the main building close, then seconds later a truck engine started up. A four-by-four came around the end of the building, flicked on its brights and eased out onto the road. We watched its taillights fade around the curve.

"There goes the watchman," I said. "So far, so good."

"So far it's stupid," said the Weasel. "We don't even have a gun."

"We don't need a gun," I told him. "Neither of us could hit anything. We just got to outthink a Neanderthal."

The truth was, I was feeling steadily less confident about what we were doing. If I'd had to choose an image to illustrate the position Geisel and I were going into, it would be a toss-up between sacrificial lamb and cornered rat.

And now that we were committed to my hastily conceived plan, the small holes I'd overlooked while explaining it to Geisel half an hour ago in my kitchen had grown big enough to swallow both of us.

"Look," I said. "Savelek calls, he gets the message. So does Conroy, 'cause he's listening in."

I knew Conroy couldn't be too far away because when Skinny had called him, he had dialled a seven-digit number. "He didn't dial 1 for long distance," I said again. "That means Conroy is right here in the valley."

"Unless you didn't count right," the Weasel countered. "You know, maybe you were a little distracted at the time."

"I counted right," I said. At least I thought I had. "Anyway, Conroy is around here somewhere. He knows we're here, he knows the stuff you gave me is here, he's going to come and get it."

"And then he's gonna kill us."

"No way."

"Sure he is. The two guys came to your place were no cops. If Conroy's hiring freelance muscle, it means he's doing something he shouldn't be doing. Is he gonna want witnesses hanging around?"

It was a possibility, but I figured I had it covered. Before we'd left my place, I had written up everything I knew and put it into a sealed envelope. Then I put the package into another envelope with a covering letter and mailed it to my old boss, the former justice minister. Conroy's name was in the write-up, along with the phone tap and the two guys with guns, all my suspicions and best guesses.

"That's our insurance," I told the Weasel.

"And if Conroy cancels our insurance? If he decides to take the three mil and run, leaving us dead? Then what?"

"Then we run like hell. It's a big mountain, lots of places to hide. Besides, what else are we going to do?"

Geisel swore. "You know the fifty grand we talked about?" he said.

"Yeah?"

"Forget it."

"No way. I got your note."

"So eat it. The deal was you hold my money until I could get out from under my problem with the mob. Well I got out from under that one, and then you put me under this one! Now I'm gonna lose my money and maybe get killed."

"Nobody's gonna get killed," I said. "We just got to stall Savelek until Conroy gets here with the cavalry."

"You got a lot of faith in this Conroy," Geisel said. "I never even met the guy."

"Shh, listen," I said.

"I don't hear anything."

"Neither do I. Let's go."

We crept down to the rear of the lodge. I listened at a window, but there was no sound. We walked around to the front. The open square was still a sea of tire-churned mud, illuminated by floodlights set on high poles.

"First thing we do," I said, "is kill all the lights."

The big front doors of the lodge were locked, so I got a rock, smashed a window and climbed through. I remembered seeing a panel of switches on the wall outside the manager's office. When I threw them, the floodlights died and the mountain went black except for the faint glow from a sliver of moon rising over Georgia Strait.

I went out onto the porch. From here I could see the lights of the Powell River pulp mill all the way across the water. A long stretch down that mainland shore was Sechelt and Miggs's Camp Second Chance. It was all very far away now.

Geisel was sitting on the lodge steps, hugging the briefcase. "Now what?" he wanted to know.

"I'm thinking," I said.

"I'd feel better if we had a gun," the Weasel said.

I remembered my earlier visit to this place and said to myself, *Why not?* To Geisel I said, "OK, you want a gun, I'll get you one."

I'd seen some tools piled near the staircase in the foyer

of the lodge. I went in, found a prybar and went back to where Geisel was waiting. "Come on," I said and led him across the square toward the bottom of the ski slopes.

There was a padlock on the chain-link fence around the little shed and another on the double doors, but the prybar made short work of both. When I threw open the doors, I could smell the grease on the thing inside.

Geisel peered into the shed's dim interior. "What is that?" he said.

"That's a 105-millimetre recoilless anti-tank rifle. And those boxes against the wall are the ammunition."

"The fuck good is that gonna do us? Savelek's not gonna be in a tank."

"If it makes him stop and slow down, it gets us time," I said. "Time is good for us."

"You're gone, you're gaga, you know that, doncha?" the Weasel said.

"Help me get it out of the shed."

That was easier to say than to do. The cannon itself weighed about four hundred kilos; the trailer with its steel armature added another hundred. Fortunately the hard-packed dirt floor of the shed was firm enough. Rocking and heaving, we got the trailer rolling and dragged it out into the night air.

The ground inside the fenced enclosure was also pretty solid and sloped in the right direction. The gun's own momentum carried us right through the open gate and onto the corrugated mud of the square.

That was where we hit a problem. The cannon had been backed into the shed muzzle first and was still pointed up-slope. Unless we could trick Lou into entering the shed, it was not going to be easy bringing the weapon to bear on him.

"We've got to slew it around, aim it at the entrance," I said.

But the ground was soft and slick, and the gun was no longer co-operating. The Weasel pushed on the barrel and I pulled on the trailer hitch. One of the wheels made a sucking sound, then the resistance gave, and the trailer rotated almost a half-turn before something stuck fast.

"Rock it," I said, and we both yanked and shoved on the hitch until the wheels came up out of their ruts and the trailer started to rumble at an angle downhill. Geisel and I were pulled forward, but we managed to hang on and drag the trailer into a useful orientation before a wheel banged into a half-buried boulder and stopped. The muzzle was pointed more or less at the resort's entrance.

"Shitbags," said the Weasel, then he cocked his head. "You hear that?"

I heard it: a car engine. I saw the reflection of lights in the woods. "He's coming," I said.

I raced back to the shed, started dragging boxes out into

the open, trying to see what was written on them and trying to remember what Betchley the site engineer had told me.

I could make out that the boxes had letters stencilled on the end. *HE* stood for high explosive, which meant shrapnel. *AT* was anti-tank, the kind that would incinerate the inside of an armoured truck.

I picked up a box with *AT* on the end and staggered toward the recoilless rifle. I could understand why the army wanted only fit young men in uniform: slinging twenty-kilo ammunition around was no task for middle-aged writers.

"Get me another one of these," I told the Weasel. "Fast!"

He slithered up the slope and dragged a box toward me. Meanwhile, I levered open the cannon's breech, tore into a waxed cardboard box and hauled out the anti-tank round.

I'd been expecting something like a big bullet, steel on one end, brass on the other. Instead it was a cardboard tube big enough to hold a half-dozen toilet-paper rolls end to end. Luckily it had an arrow painted on the side that told me which end to slide into the cannon.

I found myself wondering what kind of dunderheads the military expected to use this thing, if they didn't know which end to put into the gun without an arrow to tell them. *People like that had no business messing around with cannons,* I was thinking. Then I realized that some part of me was nattering on about the matter in an attempt to distract the rest of me from thinking about what we were doing.

Focus, I told myself and shoved the round into the hole until it wouldn't go any farther, then closed the breech and dogged it down. There was a side-mounted sight like the one on a small telescope. When I looked through it I couldn't see much, but then the image brightened as the lights of Savelek's Cadillac spilled into the resort's driveway.

He stopped just short of the mud square, left the engine running and the lights on. I couldn't see anything behind the glare.

I heard a car door slam and I hoped. Then I heard a second door close and I swore.

The hope had been that Savelek had left Mo somewhere, tied up or locked in, while he came to deal with us. The second car door closing meant that he had brought her with him.

They came out into the light from the car. I looked through the cannon's telescopic sight, focussed it in on Mo's face. I remembered how she'd looked back at the house when the two thugs had been slapping me around. She'd been scared then but she'd held herself together.

But top off the day with being kidnapped by Lou Savelek, and even Wonder Woman would be losing her grip. I could see that Mo was terrified now. Those beautiful green eyes were wide open and blank, trying not to look at the man beside her, the man with the gun.

I moved the scope toward Lou. He was calm, just standing there in his camel's-hair coat, looking around into the darkness. He hadn't yet seen us at the edge of his headlights' reach. He held some kind of pistol, letting it dangle casually, muzzle down, beside his leg.

"OK, assholes!" he shouted. "Come on out!"

I turned one of the aiming wheels on the recoilless rifle, then adjusted another one a few degrees. I took hold of the firing control.

"Hold it right there, Lou!" I yelled. "I got you covered!"

"You got me covered?" He shook his head and I knew I had failed to live up to his expectations. He peered toward where he'd heard the sound of my voice. "And I got the woman here, so don't fuck with me or I'll put one in her leg right now."

"I think we need to talk, Lou," I said. "Listen to me."

Things were not going as smoothly as he wanted them to. "No," he said, "you listen to this."

He turned toward Mo, the gun coming up. Even without the scope I could see the horror on her face. I didn't think twice about it. I squeezed the button control in my right hand.

I was expecting a boom. Instead, the cannon made a noise like a giant bone breaking, the anti-tank shell leaving an indescribable whuffling sound in its wake. The round went across the road beyond Coronado's entrance and whacked into a big cedar about ten metres above the ground. The trunk instantly exploded into smoking splinters, and the top half of the conifer fell away.

"Jesus!" said Geisel.

"Reload!" I said. He tore open another box while I cracked the breech on the cannon. There was nothing left inside but a hot stink. I grabbed the second round from the Weasel, jammed it into the gun and looked to see what Lou was doing.

If I could have been objective, if I could have been one of those ramrod-backed cadets down at Royal Roads Military College in Victoria, I might have admired the bastard's coolness under fire.

Most people, if you shoot a cannon anywhere in their direction, will probably hit the dirt and stay there at least long enough to take a really comprehensive look around. That was precisely what Mo had done. I saw her scrabbling on hands and knees to get behind the Cadillac, and I knew I would have done the same.

But Lou Savelek was the kind of crazy thug who wins battles and medals, the kind who wants to do nothing but sink his hands into the enemy's guts and scatter them around the battlefield. He was coming right at me. In the few seconds it took to get the anti-tank rifle reloaded, he had already slogged most of the way across the muddy square and was still gathering speed.

I spun the wheel to depress the gun's elevation, but Lou must have seen the muzzle move. He dodged sideways. Fat chance I could swing half a tonne of steel fast enough to track him; besides, he raised the pistol and snapped off a shot. It sizzled over my head and I hit the ground.

The Weasel had also gone flat when Lou fired, so when Savelek angled to the side to avoid the cannon's line of fire, Geisel had ended up between Lou and me. That made him the first target Savelek came to when he reached us.

The stockbroker had got to his hands and knees, and was peering into the glare from Lou's headlights when Savelek charged in from the side and booted the Weasel in the gut. I heard the air whoosh out of Geisel's lungs, even over the constant stream of profanity that the mobster chanted as he followed the first kick with a second, a third, a fourth.

I got to my feet and peered into the lights for Mo. I saw her going out of the gate down toward the logging road, half running, half stumbling on all fours. She looked back once, her face white against the dark of the trees. She'd be all right in the woods. There were plenty of places to hide. For a moment I thought about doing the same thing; Savelek was fully engaged in busting up the Weasel, and I figured I was scared enough to outrun him.

But I didn't run. I let emotion overrule the sensible part of me that wanted to crawl under something and keep still.

It wasn't that I felt sorry for Geisel — hell, it was his fault the whole thing had happened. I was mad at Lou Savelek for scaring me, but most of all, for scaring the hell out of the woman I was falling in love with. The odds were, if I'd had time to calculate them, that today's events had put the kibosh on any hopes I might have had of riding off into the sunset with Maureen Migliorini, even if I managed to get off this mountain alive.

Somebody had to pay for that. Probably it was going to be me. But before that happened, I was going to get in a lick or two. Savelek was laying his fifth kick into Geisel's belly when I threw myself at him like some kind of movie stuntman. My shoulder smacked into his breadbasket, and this time it was his lungs that I heard emptying their contents.

Savelek flew backwards down the slope with me on top, the two of us tobogganing through the mud on his fancy camel's-hair coat. The gun went clattering off against some rocks.

I've heard that good fighters plan their moves in combinations. I didn't have any such plan. As we slid to a stop, I let go of Lou's lapels to follow up the dive with a fist and caught a sharp right to the left side of my jaw. It still hurt from Paunchy's contribution.

I pushed away from Savelek, rolled farther downslope and shoved myself upright just in time for my opponent to begin raining punches on my head and shoulders. I dodged and blocked as well as I could, which wasn't all that well. I swung a couple of times, too, but all I got was air.

Lou kept up the steady flood of blasphemies and anatomical descriptions he'd started with Geisel. I was too busy to give it my full attention but I didn't think he repeated himself even once.

I slipped and went to my knees under the assault, giving the mobster an opportunity to do his party trick: his toe connected with my midsection. I felt as if I was split open. I dry-heaved, curled up around his foot and slumped down, spoiling his balance so that the second kick, aimed at my head, was just a glancing blow.

I wouldn't have been surprised if Savelek had danced on my prone body, but no new punishments arrived. I levered myself up on shaking arms and looked around. Up-slope, Weasel was on his hands and knees, puking. I looked to my side and saw Savelek a few metres away, stooping to pick up his pistol.

He wiped mud from the gun with the tail of his coat and turned toward Geisel and me. "All right, assholes," he said. "Now we're gonna ... "

"Put down the gun," said a voice from the darkness.

I rolled over and peered into the gloom behind Savelek. "Conroy?" I croaked.

But that hadn't sounded like the CLEU cop's voice. And then I was sure it wasn't when the instruction came again, very crisp, slightly accented. "Put it down or I'll kill you now."

"Fuck you!" said Savelek and fired toward the sound of the voice.

The darkness lit up. I saw the mobster silhouetted by the repetitive flash from the machine pistol that opened up from the shadows. The impacts made his body jerk like a gigged fish. The weapon was silenced; all I heard was the rapid, teeth-chattering clicks of the bolt and the sound of the bullets hitting Savelek like heavy rain spattering into dry earth.

The firing stopped — it had only been a two-second burst — and Savelek was dead. He lay on his back, head down-slope, his lifeless open eyes glistening in the dim light.

I peered into the gloom. "Conroy?" I said again.

But neither of the two men who came out of the darkness was Conroy. They weren't cops. They weren't strangers either.

The older one checked Lou's body to make sure he was dead. The other held up an Uzi-type machine gun and said, "Don't move, either of you."

Then I recognized them. "Byfield and Polowicz?" I said. "What the hell?"

The Weasel got to his feet, holding his ribs, and staggered down to where we were standing. "That's not Byfield and Polowicz," he said. "I don't know who these guys are."

"But we know who you are, Mr. Geisel," said the senior

man, the one with the lawyer's face. The younger one with the thin, hard looks kept the machine pistol trained on us.

"What's going on?" the Weasel said.

"Let's get a little uphill," said Senior, "out of this damn mud."

The junior man gestured with the gun, and Weasel and I slipped and slopped our way back to the solider ground where the cannon's trailer had lodged.

"Now," said Senior, when we were on firmer soil, "where is the material the gangster wanted?"

"It's in a briefcase in the shed up there," I said. He went to get it, flicking on a flashlight. And I started thinking, hard and fast.

I went back over what I knew about High Country Mining, about the package of bumf Geisel had given me, that I had read and then thrown away when the job literally went up in smoke. I began to get a picture that made a kind of sense.

The picture came into sharp focus when the senior man came back with the briefcase, knelt down and rooted through it under the glare of his flashlight, then said, "It's not here."

He got up and came closer, shining the light first in my face and then in the Weasel's. "I'm going to ask you this just once," he said, "and if I don't like the answer, my associate will shoot one of you in the knee. Then we'll begin again."

All at once I had heard enough to place the accent: they were South African. Now it all fit together.

"This man gave you," he said to me, "some information. I want that information."

"Was it the handwritten notes? On lab notebook paper?"

"Yes."

"I threw them away," I said.

He stepped in closer, his nose five centimetres from mine, his voice very soft. "You threw them away?"

"Yes," I said. "After the explosion. I thought the job was dead and I just tossed the background material in the garbage."

He turned away and stood with his hands in his pockets, staring at the lights of Courtenay and Comox, far down the mountain. "You wouldn't still have that garbage somewhere, would you?" he asked.

"No. They've collected since then. It's buried at the dump."

I heard him sigh. "They are really not going to like this," he said, as if to himself. But the junior one also heard and did not entirely repress a snort of contempt.

"You find it amusing?" asked Senior.

"I said we should have taken this one when he came to the Americans' place." He looked at me. "You had that material then, didn't you?"

I nodded.

"So," said Junior, gesturing with the Uzi. "None of this would have been necessary if you had taken my advice."

Senior took a deep breath, let it go. His shoulders slumped. "That will probably be in your report."

"It will."

"Well then," said the older man. "We had better tidy up and go."

That did not sound good. "Wait a minute," I said. "I think I have this thing figured out."

"How unfortunate for you," said Junior.

"The two Americans, Byfield and Polowicz, they really did come up with a way of getting platinum out of North American ore, didn't they?"

Senior's eyebrows went up. "Very good," he said. "Actually, they were part of a research group at the University of Witwatersrand. I understand they discovered some unlikely catalytic reaction that increased the leaching capacity of cyanide almost a hundredfold. Their findings legally belong to the Republic of South Africa, but they believed they would make more money on the open market."

"And you guys were sent to deal with them."

"We are from the Department of National Security. We were to bring them back to South Africa with their notes and papers. If necessary, we could bring the material and leave them behind with a warning." He sighed, then continued. "Unfortunately my young associate was a little

impetuous in his questioning of Mr. Byfield. The man suf-
fered a heart attack. Mr. Polowicz began struggling and
had to be silenced. But by then we knew they didn't have
the material."

The Weasel was following now. "They must've figured
that as long as you didn't have the notes, they could make
a deal. So they give it to me to hold onto — what do I
know? So I give it to Raff, and he throws it away."

"But you didn't know that, so you came after both of
us," I said.

"Exactly," said the senior South African.

"So the phone tap was yours," the Weasel said.

"You found it? My estimation of you two goes up."

"We didn't think it was yours," I said.

"Then whose?"

"We thought it was this cop who was interested in
Geisel," I said. "When we set up this meeting with him,"
I indicated Savelek's body, "we thought the cops would
come and save us."

"You must be very disappointed," said Junior.

I ignored the tone. "So it was you who searched my
place last week," I said.

"We also searched your car when you left it at the
airport."

"And you sent two guys to rough me up."

"It seemed best to remain in the background," said the

senior man. "Finally, however, we had to meet again. I am sorry about that."

The Weasel's danger antennae came up again. "What are you sorry for? I mean, this has all been a misunderstanding, no harm done, right?"

The senior South African looked at Savelek's corpse sprawled in the mud. "I regret," he said, "that I will already face sufficient professional embarrassment when I return home, perhaps even forced retirement."

The younger one sneered. "Our countries are not engaged in hostilities, which means our actions would scarcely be acceptable if they became public. Leaving you to talk about it would simply compound the difficulties."

"Whoa," said Geisel, backing away.

"Wait a minute," I said again.

"I think we have waited enough," said the younger one, raising the machine pistol.

"No, listen. Before we came up here tonight, we wrote up everything that's happened and mailed it off to my former employer, who used to be the Canadian minister of justice."

Senior stroked his chin. "A sensible move if you thought you were victims of a dishonest policeman. But I doubt you mentioned us."

He was right. It was desperation time. "No, there is another, very important aspect to this," I said to the senior man, "if we could just take a moment to discuss it."

He shrugged. I took it as an encouragement to keep talking. Many were the times when I had relied on a fast brain and a glib tongue to get me out of the path of trouble. But there were also the times when my talents had failed me, and I had ended up on my butt in the dust with a bloody nose and loose teeth.

This time the stakes were final. And so would be any mistakes I made. I called on the little guy in the back of my mind to wake up: we were about to put forward the argument of our life.

"Why was the formula so important?" I asked. Any good speechwriter knows never to pose a rhetorical question without answering it immediately. "Not because of the money. It's because there are only two places where platinum-group metals occur in mineable quantities." I held up one finger. "South Africa." I held up a second finger. "And the Soviet Union."

"We know this," said Junior.

"And what do we need platinum-group metals for?" Again I answered myself. "To make jet engines and light-weight steel alloys for the military. So, without South African minerals, NATO goes down the tubes, the Russians win the cold war and the Kremlin rules the world."

"Very good," said Senior, "but I think you should come to the point soon. We have much to do."

"The point is this," I said. "The Russians *don't* win the

cold war because the cold war is *over*. The Poles, the Czechs, the Hungarians, they're all opting out. Even the East Germans are pouring over the border. I bet the Berlin Wall is down within a year."

The younger one snorted impatiently, but the older man was still willing to listen. I poured it on.

"Russia is flat broke. Gorbachev is begging the Americans and the Europeans for investment, if not outright foreign aid. So those supplies of strategic minerals are soon going to be available to anybody with a chequebook."

"So?" said the younger one.

"So it's a downshift. The whole world is shifting down to a lower gear, and who needs South Africa?" I said.

"You little liberal prick," Junior said and raised the gun again, but the older man put his hand on the barrel and pushed it down.

"You're saying none of this matters?" he said.

"Of course it matters. But it's *done!* I'm saying you've been so good at your job that you've finished the work. Communism is dying. The cold war is over. You won. And that means South Africa no longer has any strategic value to the west."

"That is pigshit!" hissed the younger one, but his partner ran his hand over his face and stared at the lights of town.

"On the other hand," I said, as unobtrusively as possible, "there are three million dollars on this mountain. Enough to buy a deservedly decent retirement for a couple of successful cold warriors."

"Those papers in the briefcase?" said Senior.

"Bearer bonds. Same as cash," I said. I looked at the Weasel to see if he was going to make a noise about it, but he kept his eyes on Junior's gun.

I'd gotten the older man to thinking, but the young one was not the type. "We are Afrikaner officers of the Department of National Security," he sneered. "We do what we do for the destiny of our race, not for money. You North Americans need to learn that some people can't be bought."

"I'm afraid he's right," said Senior. "But we'll take the money anyway, as a contribution to the national treasury."

Junior chuckled. "Unfortunately it won't make up for the billions that new leaching catalyst would have been worth."

The older one sighed. He still looked thoughtful. "Janny," he said, "would you come up here and collect the briefcase while I take care of things?"

The younger one backed up the hill, the machine pistol still trained on the Weasel and me. Senior moved right behind the cannon. I saw him reach for something.

Then, as his young partner came level with the exhaust slots just forward of the thick steel breech block, the older man closed his hand on the firing button and launched the

105-millimetre anti-tank shell into the ground in front of Lou's Cadillac.

A fountain of mud and gravel shot into the air behind Geisel and me, but we didn't notice. Our eyes were on the gun-toting junior South African as the full force of the cordite charge was vented sideways out of the perforated breech block at the base of the recoilless rifle. The cannon blast tore Janny's head into shards of bone and sprayed his blood and brains into a mist of droplets that dissipated across the mud.

Ten

THE ECHOES OF THE BLAST were still reverberating
from the hillside, and the dead man's body was still slump-
ing to the ground. I jumped for the machine pistol that
had fallen from Janny's lifeless hands. Too late. Senior was
pointing an efficient looking automatic handgun at me.

"Mr. Rafferty, you are not the type," he said. He was
the fifth person in the past two days who had pointed a
gun at me but at least he seemed to be of two minds about
using it.

Then he made up his mind. "I am not a greedy man,"
he said. "I will only take half."

I had to give credit to the Weasel. He swallowed the
bleat before it was even half-formed, then sighed and said,
"Okay."

I held the flashlight while they divided it up. The South
African kept the briefcase and the guns. "Thank you,
gentlemen," he said and turned to leave.

The Weasel clutched the wad of bearer bonds to his chest. "You guys," he said, "we do have one other problem."

"What's that?" we both asked.

He directed his answer to me. "Your girlfriend. She knows that you and I were up here with Savelek. Now he's dead and we're not, and she's probably planning to say something about this to the police. That's when my name and the three million bucks are gonna come up and a lot of people are gonna want to talk to me. Including Lou's uncle."

"Where is this young lady?" said the South African, looking around.

"She ran into the woods before you arrived," I said.

"Ah," he said. "I don't suppose you'd want me to ... " he gestured with the pistol.

"No!" I said. "I'm sure I can make her see reason."

"I'm not," said Geisel. "A lot of what's been happening around here has not been too reasonable."

"If you need to disappear, I can perhaps be of assistance," said the South African.

"Would you?" said Geisel.

"Why not? You are, in a very real sense, my benefactor. I feel an obligation. Also, in the interests of self-preservation, I would not like you to have discuss these matters with the police — at least not before I have put certain events into motion." He thought for a moment, then said, "Here's what we'll do."

Under his direction, Geisel emptied his pockets and stuffed the contents into those of the dead South African. They were roughly matched in height and weight.

"What about fingerprints?" the Weasel wanted to know.

"There shouldn't be any," said the agent and had us drag Savelek and the other corpse down to Lou's car. We arranged the bodies in the front seat, strapping them in with seat belts. Handling the headless South African was a messy business, but we eventually got him settled.

The older man brought down a couple of boxes marked *HE* and put them in the Cadillac's back seat. "That should do it," he said. "Stand clear."

We followed him back up the slope to the recoilless rifle, where he loaded in a high-explosive round, sighted and adjusted the controls. He looked up from the sight, said, "Goodbye, Janny, you little shit," and fired.

The shell crashed into the Cadillac's hood and instantly exploded. The big car leapt several metres into the air, flame spewing from its blown-out windows. Before it landed, the rounds in the back seat cooked off, and the double detonation ripped the vehicle into chunks of smoking metal.

A six-metre fireball flumed up into the air on a column of black smoke. The noise was like climbing into an oil drum, pulling down the lid and lighting the biggest, baddest firecracker of your whole childhood.

"We should leave now," said the South African. "This is bound to command some attention."

There wasn't a big hurry. It would take the volunteer firefighters down in Courtenay a while to get their pants on and work their way up into the bush.

The South African had a four-wheel drive truck parked a few hundred metres down the road, near where I'd left the Concord. I watched him and the Weasel drive away on one of the subsidiary logging roads that branched off the Mount Washington main. They would come back to civilization farther up the valley, emerging in the farming community of Merville.

I was not leaving, however. When their tail lights went out of sight, I played the flashlight the South African had given me among the trees lining the logging road. "Mo!" I called. "It's me, Raff! It's all over. You can come out."

But she didn't come out. And it was a while before I found her. There were footprints in the soft earth beside the logging road, then I saw where she had gone into the undergrowth, blindly fleeing the terror at Coronado. I followed the trail of snapped twigs and crushed branches where she had pushed through a thicket.

Twenty metres in from the road, I came upon her. She was sitting against a stump. Her clothes were muddy and there were leaves in her hair. She stared into the beam of light, but I don't think she saw me. Or anything.

I knelt and put my arm around her shoulders. "It's all right," I said.

She began to shake. "I can't handle this," she said at last, through chattering teeth.

"It's over," I said. I pulled her close to me and held her until the shivers subsided.

"Raff, I just want to go home," she said.

"There's an early plane at 7:30."

"I don't like feeling like this."

"It'll be all right," I said, again. As if saying it would make it so.

But it wasn't all right, and I didn't know if it ever would be again.

All the way down the dark forest road and out onto the highway where we saw the yellow fire engines screaming toward the turnoff, she said nothing. She spoke only one word to me, and that was when I opened the car door and reached for her arm to help her out.

"Don't," was all she said.

She went into the house, sat where she had sat only hours before with the shotgun pointed at her head. I brought her a couple of Valium left over from the time when I thought diazepam might substitute for normal human existence.

She chased down the pills with water, then when I

suggested she should sleep, let me lead her to the bedroom. She lay down, still muddy, on top of the covers. I put a quilt over her and brought a chair so I could sit beside the bed until her breathing told me she had fallen asleep.

I slept finally on the carpet beside the bed, to be awakened around four-thirty. She was talking in her sleep, warning someone or something to get away. She dropped off again, and so did I.

Sometime around seven, I woke fast, falling out of sleep with a shock. The bed was empty. I got up and searched the house, then looked out the front window in time to see a cab taking her away.

I opened the door, but by then the car had turned the corner. I saw her through the rear window. She didn't look back.

Later I called the number she had given me, the one at her apartment in Vancouver, but got an answering machine. The third time I left a message.

I also tried several times to get through to Miggs's place in Sechelt, but there was no answer there all day. Late in the evening I tried again.

Miggs picked up the phone.

"Listen, man," he said. "I don't know what you did to her, but she doesn't want to hear from you or about you. And if I ever get within arm's reach of you, I won't be the only one needs a wheelchair." And he hung up.

It was no use telling the dead line that I hadn't meant to hurt her, that I was almost as much a victim as she was. Even if Miggs had been listening, even if I'd called up all my professional glibness, I doubted I could have convinced him. I didn't believe it myself.

A speechwriter knows that the key to making a good argument is first to believe what you're saying. Even if you're writing for a speaker whose take on the world is diametrically opposed to your own convictions, you have to absorb it, believe in it, see the universe through the speaker's eyes at least long enough to get the words lined up.

George Orwell described in *1984* the ability to hold two contradictory points of view and to believe both at the same time. He called it doublethink. Freelance speechwriters can get pretty good at it — although it sometimes leaves a bad taste in the mind.

But I couldn't argue with Miggs's assessment of me. I'd blown it, the way I always blew it. Lost the girl and lost the respect of one of the few people I'd ever truly admired.

I reread the story about the local RCMP identifying Geisel's body and sipped my tea. Three days had passed since I had brought Maureen Migliorini back down from the mountain and put her to bed.

So I waited. I'd turned out to be pretty good at that. The day after the story ran in the local paper, Conroy the CLEU cop came by, asked me a lot of questions about Geisel and noted down my unhelpful answers. I had the impression he wasn't thirsting to bring Lou Savelek's killer to justice.

The morning after Conroy's visit, Karen phoned to tell me that Pastorel had called an emergency meeting of Miggs's campaign backers. A plane ticket was waiting at the airport.

I caught the early afternoon Air BC flight. It was a Twin Otter, the smaller version of the big Buffalo used for search and rescue flights. It was loud and bouncy but it put me down at Vancouver International Airport in thirty-five minutes. The cab ride downtown took longer.

An assistant led me to Pastorel's private office. It was the first time I had seen it, and I wasn't surprised to find a trophy wall of plaques, certificates and framed grip-and-grin shots of Lyle being toothy next to politicians and media celebrities.

My ex-wife and her husband were on the couch. Walter Fornoy was next to them, looking at his watch. Fritz Gershom was at the corner window looking out over the harbour, and Bas Cowper was sitting at a round table surrounded by chairs. I said hello to them generally and joined Bas.

I raised my eyebrows at him in the "what's up?" mode, but he just shrugged.

The assistant who had shown me in left and came back with a television and VCR on a wheeled cart. He plugged it in, tested that everything was ready to go, then left us at a signal from Pastorel.

Fornoy looked at his watch again, growing impatient now, then Lloyd Mackenzie stepped into the room, apologizing for being late. Pastorel waved him to a seat next to Cowper and me. Gershom preferred to stand.

There was an uncomfortable silence. Pastorel cleared his throat and said, "I'm afraid this is not a happy occasion. What I'm about to show you arrived this morning by messenger. It's self-explanatory."

He went to his desk, unlocked a drawer and removed a videotape, which he inserted into the machine. He turned on the TV. The screen went from snow to black, then up came the images.

It was rough footage, roughly edited, with no narration, but it was eloquent enough. There were shots of Miggs, some of them apparently dubbed from news broadcasts. Then there were shots of Pastorel and of Karen at receptions and other public events with some of the people whose photographs graced the wall across from me.

Then there was a series of quick shots: stills and footage of people getting out of cars or walking down sidewalks.

The common denominator was that each shot ended with its subject walking into Pastorel's building.

The images were sometimes jerky, sometimes framed by abbreviated curtains hanging in the window of a VW bus. But Fornoy and Gershom were recognizable. So were Mackenzie and Cowper. So was I.

Now there was a travelling shot as the camera came across the street and into the building we had each been seen to enter. Then it tracked to the directory in the lobby and zoomed in on the listing that included Pastorel's name.

A jump cut took us to the hallway outside Pastorel's suite of offices, to the gilt-lettered sign on the hardwood door.

Then the perspective altered. There was a shaky long shot of Pastorel's building. I looked to the windows and realized that it had been taken from the elevated parking garage across the street.

The long shot steadied, then zoomed in on the corner windows. The faces were recognizable even through the glass. And now we got sound:

"So what we need here is somebody else, somebody without an existing power base within the party, somebody who can rally support from all camps, somebody who can take over the party," said Pastorel on the tape. His voice was tinny but the oily smugness came through intact.

"And that somebody is Tony Migliorini," Karen said and

went on to talk about the focus group research, about how Miggs tested so well in key demographics.

"Is he maybe too good to be true?" asked Gershom.

"Is he controllable?" That was Fornoy.

It went on for another few minutes. There was the carved sign at Camp Second Chance. There was me walking and talking with Maureen, roughly intercut with images of me sitting with Pastorel and Karen. There was a shot of me through my office window, my fingers pounding away on the keyboard, writing Miggs's speech.

Then there was Karen and me framed by the window of the Hotel Vancouver's Spanish Grill.

"He's just to get the ball rolling, isn't he?" That was my voice. "So who's the real client? Amazing Grace? Bud Smith?"

The tape had the sound of Karen's laughter. "Doesn't matter. In fact it's none of the above. We don't have a client. We just need to break the stalemate, get a leadership campaign going. There'll be plenty of work after that."

"But if the big guns don't support Miggs, he'll get ground into hamburger." Me again.

"If his campaign stalls, he can throw his support behind one of the front-runners," said Karen's taped voice.

The tape ended on a homemade title card, block capitals picked out in Letraset. *ANATOMY OF A CONSPIRACY*, it read. After that, the screen went to black and then to snow.

Pastorel switched it off. There was silence in the room. Then Mackenzie asked, "Is it a Zalmoid thing?"

Karen shook her head. "That was our first thought. But it's not about that."

"Then how much is it about?" asked Gershom.

"A hundred thousand."

Mackenzie said, "Who did it?"

"Gilfillan," I said. "Nestor Gilfillan, ace detective and budding extortionist."

Pastorel's eyes widened. "How did you know?" he said.

I told them about pulling him out from under the hedge in Sechelt and the licence plate. I didn't mention Skinny and Paunchy: none of that footage had shown up in the video.

Fornoy said, "It doesn't matter who the guy is or what kind of axe he's grinding. We pay him and make sure he goes away."

Gershom nodded. The industry PR reps shrugged. Pastorel looked at his shoes. "He wants cash," he said.

Gershom said, "I'm pretty liquid this week. I'll put together the money, you guys can pay in later. But Lyle ... "

Pastorel looked up. "Yeah?"

"When you pay this asshole, make your own video of the payoff and send me a copy. We don't want this guy coming back for more."

Bas Cowper looked out the window, his elbows on the

table, his chin in his hands. "Christ," he said. "You know what the worst part is? We're stuck with Vander Zalm. And that Dutchman's going to screw it all up for all of us."

Pastorel was punching Miggs's number into the speaker phone. I heard it ring far off in Sechelt, then Mo's voice answered.

My flinch was a minuscule movement, but my ex-wife knew me well. She cocked her head and raised an eyebrow. I looked away.

Her husband asked for Miggs and waited for him to come on the line. I watched my feet and listened. I had to admire Pastorel's sheer professionalism, the way I had to admire the predatory efficiency of a tiger shark. From his upbeat, used-car-salesman's tone of voice, no one could have guessed that all his plans had just been squished into a gelatinous mess and dropped ten storeys to splatter all over the parking lot.

Eventually, he worked his way around to the nub of his message. "Thing is," he told Miggs, "we may have to take a pass on the speaking tour. Window of opportunity has shrunk. Some wrinkles in the financing arrangements, can't get all the ducks in a row. You know how it is."

Miggs was silent for a beat, then he said, "You're saying you want to back out?"

"No, it's not that we want to, Miggs," Pastorel lied, "it's a matter of coordination, a logistics thing. You understand."

"No, I don't understand," came the voice from the speaker phone, "but I don't really care. Fact is, I had my doubts from the beginning, and that guy you sent over here only confirmed them. Count me out."

There was a click as he hung up. Now everybody was looking at me.

I lifted my head. "Some people are just not right for politics," I said.

A week later I sent Mo a letter care of Camp Second Chance. It was the fifteenth or sixteenth draft. I didn't know how to say what I had to say, and it had got to the point where I was just chasing words around the computer screen and losing my mind.

This was not a time to play wordsmith. So I erased the text yet again and just tried to put down the simple truth. I needed her. I had put her through hell without meaning to. I begged her not to push me away.

I mailed it and waited. A lot of days went by. I wandered around the house and the neighbourhood, explaining to myself in detail the several instances where I had let things get totally out of control.

It was a Tuesday. The front page of the Victoria daily showed East German police knocking down the Berlin Wall, aided by laughing volunteers from the west. Inside, a brief

item noted that the four dissident MLAs had abandoned
their exile and come home to the Socred caucus, wagging
their tails behind them. The political columnists all agreed
that the fizzling of the anti-Vander Zalm revolt ended the
party's last chance to win the next election. Now it was
more a question of whether or not there would be any
Social Credit Party left once the electorate got their hands
on some ballots.

I decided I would stick to corporate work and leave
politics to Karen. By the time I had finished the daily and
the locals, the mail had come: a History Book Club flyer,
a big brown envelope with a U.S. stamp and a letter post-
marked Sechelt. I took the letter into the kitchen, put
it on the table and looked at it for a long time before I
opened it.

On a single sheet of paper she had written, "I don't know.
Maybe in a month or two, but don't try so hard." And
below that it said, "Love, Mo."

I started breathing again. I made myself a pot of tea,
sat at the table and read and reread the sixteen words.
Then I looked out the window at the autumn sun on the
glacier.

This time I hadn't lost it all. There was a chance, and I
would take it. "It'll be all right," I told myself. I didn't even
add a "maybe."

I picked up the big brown envelope. Its postmark was

the U.S. Virgin Islands. When I opened it, out fell a bearer bond for twenty-five thousand dollars and a note. The note read, "Half of your fifty went to you-know-who. We're square."